Beyond the Cogs

A Steampunk Anthology

C. Vonzale Lewis
Nicholas J. Evans
Elle Beaumont

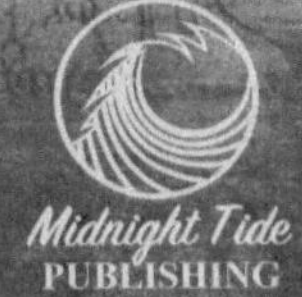

Midnight Tide
PUBLISHING

BEYOND THE COGS

Copyright © 2021 by C. Vonzale Lewis, Nicholas J. Evans, Elle Beaumont

Midnight Tide
PUBLISHING

Published by Midnight Tide Publishing.
www.midnighttidepublishing.com

Cover designed by Stars Cold Night
www.bookcoversrealm.com

This is a work of fiction. Names, characters, brands, trademarks, places, and incidents either are the product of the author's imagination or are used fictitiously. Any resemblance to actual events, locales, organizations, or persons, living or dead, is entirely coincidental and beyond the intent of either the author or the publisher.

All rights reserved, which includes the right to reproduce this book or portions thereof in any form whatsoever except as provided by the U.S. Copyright Law.

Look to the skies and stay adventurous, my friends!

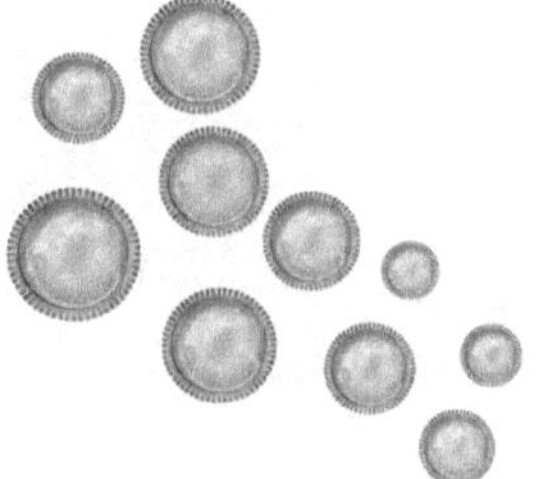

THE SOULLESS ONES
BY C. VONZALE LEWIS

In 1901, a doctor named Duncan MacDougall tried to prove the existence of the human soul. He concluded it weighed...21 grams.

Night draped over the city of New Orleans like an unwanted lover. The crescent moon hung over the crescent city, fighting to gain some purchase, but the night was winning. Even the muted light from the gas lamps barely outlined the cobblestone in front of me.

I didn't mind the night. The creatures of legend I usually hunted preferred its sweet embrace. But tonight, I wasn't looking for monsters. Tonight, I was searching for Frank Covington. A man who had stolen from the wrong person and I was tasked with bringing him in dead or alive.

And my weeklong pursuit had led me here.

Bourbon Street stretched out before me. Deserted. An eerie feeling chewed on my bones and settled in my gut. I'd been to New Orleans a time or two in the past and had never seen it like this. Quiet. As if everyone had picked up and moved on.

Something was off.

The gears on my horse, Betsy, clanged as she switched from mammal to machine. When my grandfather designed her, he gave her the ability to switch at will. All of her mechanics lay tucked away in the thick folds of her flesh. She looked like any other dark brown mustang, until she changed. She only switched to machine when she was spooked, or I asked her to.

A warm breeze carrying the stench of old garbage and stale water, ruffled my braid, blowing through the strands of hair around my face. I blinked a few times, to ease the sting in my eyes.

Betsy's red gaze cut through the dark and highlighted the rancid puddles along the streets making them look like blood had been spilt.

"Well, Parasol, looks like we scared the locals," my sister Pearl announced. "You think we'll find Covington here?" Pearl's footsteps sounded like an automaton invasion. Each of her footfalls seemed more menacing than the next. She could move silently if she wanted, but she obviously had the same strange feeling Betsy and I had; something wasn't quite right *and* Pearl wanted to make her presence known. "We should keep going. Nothing good is going to come of this place." She turned her head and took in the deposits of water along the street. "Looks like they're trying to give birth to another plague."

"You sound paranoid," I told her.

"And you've gone blind." From one step to the next, she silenced her footfalls. "I might rust," she said with a sigh.

I'd offered to get her a horse, but she refused to ride it. She preferred to walk beside me. And Pearl would never rust. The alloy my grandfather used when he built her repelled all the elements.

Pearl had been a gift from my grandfather when I was three. I'd wanted a little sister. But my mother, having suffered a massive hemorrhage when giving birth to me, couldn't have any more kids. Pearl seemed like the next best thing. And she really was. My constant companion, and at times, a pain in my ass. As well as a hypochondriac.

"You know you won't rust," I answered, focusing back on the street. Pearl sighed and walked on.

I glanced over at the building on my right. A bar whose French doors lay open giving me a view of the darkness inside. The green shutters had been ravaged by time. But still the building held on.

The structure next to it had been built recently, a tall gray brick building stretching up to the sky. The sign on front read: Josephine's Place. From the looks of it, it probably served as both an eatery and place to stay.

Pearl scanned the building. "A lot of people are holed up inside."

I gave a non-committal noise still staring at the building. "How many?" I asked, finally.

"I count sixty. All huddled together on the bottom floor. Maybe they're having a party."

I shook my head. "No. It's too quiet."

The building next to it, an apothecary shop had a light on somewhere in the back. I strained to see into the darkness but all I could make out were the clay pots and burners used for mixing herbs in the display window.

"I count two inside the shop," Pearl said.

I pushed Betsy on and took in the rest of the buildings in the once thriving French Quarter. What used to be a street crammed with strip clubs, bars, and restaurants now housed most of the city of New Orleans. Only a few areas outside of the quarter remained. And the once residential areas had been turned into a bayou.

A hundred years ago, at the end of the 21st century, humanity learned the hard way that Mother Nature was real. Tired of humanity's efforts to destroy her, she sent a great plague across the world, wiping out over half the population. Even technology suffered when a madman, believing he had been ordained by the deity herself, released a virus into the computer network, killing all of mankind's tech instantly. The speed in which the virus spread, left Cyber experts unable to undo the damage—sending mankind's technology back into the stone ages.

The oceans rose, swallowing the coastlines and depositing waste onto the sandy shores. It was as if the sea had vomited up hundreds of years' worth of trash, cleansing it in one massive wave—blocking our access to the water. All the speculation about California being swallowed by the ocean one day turned out to be wrong. It was the southern coastlines that paid the largest price. Giving up their land to the icy blue depths as if in sacrifice.

It took almost fifty years for humanity to reclaim its coastlines, giving us access to the ocean once again.

Fires had raged, leaving behind endless wastelands and

only a few old buildings managed to escape the inferno. New life shoved its way out of the scorched earth, healthy and strong. Once the last embers had died out, previously extinct plants came back with a vengeance, giving humanity access to ancient healing that had been lost to it for thousands of years.

After a short period of uncertainty and fear, humanity clawed its way back from that devastation and rebuilt the cities and reclaimed the land. Building structures inspired by both the Victorian era and the Wild West, mixing them in with the crumbling buildings from the 21st century. A jarring mishmash in a society that could not seem to decide on what it wanted to be.

I hoped it would settle back into the Victorian age. I rather liked the stone buildings. Less chance of it all crumbling down again. And from what I've seen of the architecture of the 21st century, it couldn't hold a candle to Victorian beauty.

Betsy clopped along, her hooves clacking against the stone, sending an echo down the deserted street.

A swath of light from a building farther up, shone on the ground, cutting through the darkness. Maybe someone was open.

A community barn loomed up ahead. The wooden sign had a crude drawing of a horse on it. It swayed in the briny breeze that blew over the street—its hinges creaking, mixing in with the rush of warm wind. I glanced up at the sky and watched as the rain clouds rolled slowly over the city, covering the sliver of a moon. I'd hope to find shelter before the storm came in. Looks like I'd made it just in time.

"Are we stopping?" Pearl asked.

"Yeah. We might as well take shelter and continue searching in the morning." I glanced over my shoulder. "It will give our tail time to show himself."

Pearl came to a full stop, turning the top part of her body around in that eerie way she did. She had a mixture of both humanoid and mechanical parts and looked like a woman stuck inside of a soup can with two shapely arms and legs and two small mounds fashioned in front to resemble breasts.

Her facial structure resembled the family's: doe-shaped eyes and full lips. My mother had sewn together a wig of long black hair to run down her back like ours. When I was older, I'd tried to paint her a russet brown color like me. I'd learned two things from that misguided attempt. One, you couldn't put regular paint on alloy and hope it looked real. And two, Pearl had also been programmed with a personality like my grandfather's based on the long-suffering sighs she gave me while I was painting her.

She never removed the paint, leaving one of her arms to resemble a battle wound.

She was the first model my grandfather built that could, except for her torso, pass for human.

Pearl stared down the street. "He's a crafty one. I still think you should have let me go and introduce myself." Whoever the stranger was, he did not want Pearl introducing herself. There would be nothing left when she was done with him.

"No. Let him come to us." I was more than a little curious to meet the dumbass who had decided to follow me across the New Collective.

"You think Blankeon sent him to keep tabs on you?" Pearl asked.

"I don't know," I said, thinking. I wouldn't be surprised if he had. It was taking me much longer than usual to bring in my bounty. Blankeon wasn't a patient man. And he was not above withholding the rest of my money out of spite alone. Especially if he felt I didn't complete the job in a timely manner. Which would lead to an altercation, leaving one of the few people who were willing to hire me dead.

When I'd first started my trade, very few would hire me. And those who even entertained a meeting with me usually ended up laughing in my face. The laughter always died when I plowed my fists into their faces. My honor might have been avenged, but that didn't leave me with a job. So, I had to keep Blankeon happy. And that meant bringing in Covington. Dead or alive. I was leaning more toward dead. He'd caused me enough hassle. And I had no plans to drag him back across the unforgiving terrain still kicking.

Betsy jerked at her reins. I rubbed her neck to calm her.

A figure stepped out of the shadows. Over six feet, wearing a wide-brimmed black hat, his long coat bellowed—exposing a revolver on his hip—as he moved on silent footsteps toward us. I pulled my SIG pistol from its holster on my left thigh and pointed it in his direction.

"Easy now," the man said. "Just come to give you a warning."

"Oh, I don't like the sound of that," Pearl said, and shined her scope in his dark green eyes. He shielded his face, twisting his mouth into an ugly sneer. A few days' worth of stubble rested on his weather-worn skin.

Underneath the coat, he wore dark leather pants and a black shirt with silver buttons. His dark eyes continued to assess me and Pearl. Probably looking for weakness. He wouldn't find any. While my SIG pistol could put a lovely hole in all that black, Pearl would rip his heart out of his chest with minimal effort.

Finally, he raised his hands as if trying to show that he meant me no harm. Pearl moved closer to him, and I let the gun rest by my side. After a brief hesitation, he let his arms fall. He gave Pearl a wary glance and then focused back on me. "Sheriff has imposed a curfew. I just wanted to make sure you were aware." The way he said "sheriff" gave me the impression he didn't much care for the man.

"Does that curfew extend to you as well?"

He sneered. "The sheriff likes to think it does."

Betsy shifted, restless. I gave her a soothing pat and climbed down so I could face the stranger. I shoved my pistol back in its holster and stepped toward him. "What happened here?"

He paused, giving me a once over, his gaze finally

settling on my face. "A family out near on the bayou was found dead last night. Some believe it was wild animals." He looked down the street. "But we all know a Soulless One has come to town."

Not good. A Soulless One—especially the newly turned—could level an entire town before it satiated its thirst. And yes, their kills resembled an animal attack. All except for the fang marks in the neck. The telltale sign of the Soulless One's kill. It was also the basis for the vampiric myth of blood drinking.

"If you think a Soulless One is roaming the streets, why are you out here in the open?" I asked.

He gave me a twisted smile. "Me and my boys are hunting it. Doing that worthless sheriff's job. Instead of making everyone stay inside, he should have rounded up a few of us to help flush out that evil son of a bitch! Instead, him and his deputies sit behind locked doors, hiding. Protecting their own asses."

Idiots. The only thing they would be able to do was piss it off before it tore into them, seeking their souls.

"Do you even know how to kill one?" I asked. It was a stupid question. But if I could dissuade this idiot from setting out on a suicide mission, I would.

He pulled a gun from his hip and opened the cylinder, showing me a row of silver bullets.

I sighed. "Silver alone won't kill it."

His face scrunched up. "What do you know?" he asked, his tone suggesting he thought I was clueless. I was surprised when he didn't start waxing on about how to kill a Soulless One. About all his vast knowledge on the subject. I'd run into a few people just like him. All of them dead now.

I sighed again and turned from him—unable to keep the disgust and frustration off my face. I glanced down the way we came. If sixty people were holed up inside of Josephine's, maybe they believed there was a Soulless One roaming the streets as well.

I cursed inwardly. Of course, my pursuit of Frank would lead me here. To the very things I usually hunted. Coincidence? I didn't know.

I wanted to tell the idiot to go inside. To explain to him how the Soulless were really killed. But telling him that would put me in danger. Some secrets just could not be told. And even if they did learn how, they wouldn't be able to obtain the means to do so.

Besides, the twisted sneer on his face told me I'd be wasting my time anyway. If he and his boys wanted to hunt down a Soulless One, despite the stories of others who had set out on a similar pursuit and ended up dead, then nothing I said would stop them.

I looked up at the sign. "This your stable?"

He spat on the ground and slid his hands in his pockets, a mixture of nonchalance and defiance in his body language. "No," he said finally. "Carl Stevens owns the place. You can board your horse there tonight and settle up with him in the morning."

I jerked my head back toward Josephine's Place. "Is the hotel full?"

He glanced at the aforementioned place; a quizzical look crossed his face. "Only place taking guests is Willow Sin at the end of street," he said, not looking at me. "Strange that," he added as if he were talking to himself.

"Why?" I asked.

He turned back to me. "Why what?"

"Why is it strange Josephine's isn't taking guests?"

He shrugged, dismissing the question. My curiosity was piqued. Could be the hotel was full, given the number of people inside. But something in his behavior felt off. Like he couldn't understand why Josephine's wasn't open either.

I pointed at Willow Sin. "Why send me to a brothel?" There had to be other hotels in town.

He gave me a mischievous look, his eyes roaming down the length of my body. "Because you should fit in nicely."

"Parasol, I do believe this rattlesnake called you a hooker." Pearl moved forward. "Where are my manners." She extended her hand.

"Pearl," I warned, "leave it."

She turned and gave me a look loaded with frustration. She knew I could take care of myself. But it didn't matter. Despite her being technically younger than me, Pearl liked to think of herself as my big sister. Always ready to jump in and defend my honor. The one time I did let her come to my defense, the man had ended up in a coma for a month. And I had to pay the hospital bills or end up in jail.

I pulled the picture of Covington from my pocket and showed it to the stranger. "Have you seen him in town?"

He glanced at the picture then back at me. "You a bounty hunter?" he asked, his voice heavy with sarcasm.

I didn't answer. Just kept my gaze steady on him, waiting.

Men, even in this century, still believed women were good for only a few things: cleaning, cooking, warming their sheets, and birthing their children. While I would love to show him just how wrong his thinking was, I had a job to do.

"He came through here yesterday. Bought up all the relics from the 21st century at Pat's, then spent some money at Willow Sin." He gave me a half smile. "Man liked to wave his money around. Warned him he could get robbed that way."

Seems this man loved to warn people. And I got the impression the man in front of me would have been the one to rob him.

I still couldn't figure out why Covington was spending all his money on items from the past? More importantly, what was he doing with them? As far as I knew, he only had a single horse to carry them with. When I questioned the people in the last town, they said they didn't see him carrying anything. Only buying new items. Was he trading them? Stashing them somewhere?

"Is he staying in town?" I asked.

He shook his head. "Haven't seen him today."

I thanked him for his time, took Betsy's reigns, and led

her toward the barn. A part of me wanted to try and save the foolish men who had elected themselves as Orleans' posse. Afterall, it was what I did. But I couldn't risk it.

"You pondering helping them?" Pearl asked, reading my mind.

I shook my head.

"Good. You can't fix stupid, Parasol. No matter how hard you try."

She was right, of course. Nothing I did or said, besides joining his ragtag group, would help him.

Which meant he and his boys would be dead by morning.

We stepped inside the barn. My boots crunched on the woodchips scattered across the floor, stirring up dust that danced in the meager light. I scanned the rectangular room. It had seen better days. Gouges made by both man and horse riddled the walls in a maddening pattern and long streaks marred the rough wooden floorboards. It was as if at some point, someone or something had attempted to claw its way out of the confined space. A few holes in the walls let in the briny scent from the bayou as well as the muggy heat to mix with the scent of horses and hay. Nine individual stalls—three currently occupied—were set against the back wall, and a grooming area sat directly in front.

I led Betsy to the water trough and removed my bags

while she drank. Everything I owned was contained in those three bags. One for ammunition and weapons, one for personal effects, and one for the few articles of clothing I owned—mostly jeans and a few tops. I opened my ammunition bag and pulled out a small, slender black case. Red velvet lined the inside. A dual-barreled gun rested inside, along with five silver bullets and five transparent capsules made from Aquagold and silver alloy. Three vials of a substance that allowed me to see the Soulless also lay inside.

Each capsule held 21 grams of a burnt-orange mist. The stolen soul of a Soulless Ones victim. This mist escaped the Soulless One when they were killed. My grandfather had given me twenty a month ago. I'd need to send word for more.

A horse in the nearest stall rose and kicked his door. The metal hinges rattled but held.

"Might be better to put Betsy in the back," Pearl said.

Other horses could sense the strangeness in Betsy. Not able to make out what she was, their first instinct was to attack—leading to Betsy defending herself.

I walked Betsy to a stall near the back, away from the other horses. Pearl followed me. From her silence, I could tell she was working her way up to something and, given what the stranger had said, I could guess what it was. I, too, was struggling with my initial feelings on not helping.

Once I'd secured Betsy in the stall, I pulled an apple from my bag and fed it to her. It was the only thing she could eat. The arsenic in the seeds was the only thing she could digest due to her mechanical parts. Although she has chewed on a few people a time or two. But only when she sensed them as a threat. Unable to take Pearl's silence anymore, I turned to my mechanical sister, lifting a single eyebrow in question.

She stared at me for a bit, her thoughts cycling. "We might have to hunt the Soulless One," she finally said, resignation in her voice.

She was right. Despite both our resolves to allow the idiots in town to march willingly to their own deaths, we knew we couldn't leave unless the Soulless One had been dealt with. My only issue was, once I got involved, I risked exposing my, and my grandfather's, secrets.

The Soulless Ones were beings that had lived on this earth for thousands of years. The original? Some called him the first murderer. The first-born son of Adam and Eve. While he did slay his brother, it wasn't out of jealousy. He had bargained away his soul, and when the torment and pain set in, he killed his brother and took his soul to ease his suffering.

Many theories on how to kill a Soulless One have surfaced over the years. These ideas have reduced them to vampires who drank blood, hid in coffins during the day, had an aversion to silver and garlic, and couldn't cast a reflection in the mirror.

The hypothesis about silver was only partially true. The only way silver could kill them was if it were used along with the stolen soul from a dying Soulless One. And the only way to obtain the soul was to kill a Soulless One and extract it.

They didn't feed on blood. The Soulless Ones fed on souls. Having lost their own, they were in a constant state of pain. A newly turned one could mow through an entire town trying to satiate their thirst. But the older ones had learned to live with the pain. Learned to only feed when necessary. Learned to make the souls they consumed last longer. And they were the only ones who had the strength and control to make new ones.

Of course, if one didn't have any ammo to kill them, one could try severing their head. Sadly, a few had tried and ended up being food instead. No, a beheading would only work if the Soulless One were weak and caught off guard. Not a scenario anyone should bet on. And when all else failed, fire would work. But you had to wait till the flames died down to finish them off. Otherwise, they could rise again.

I secured my bag over my shoulder. Pearl followed me out of the barn, waiting for me to answer. I needed to come up with a strategy. One that would ensure I could bring down the Soulless One with what I had. Now, I just had to hope there was only one of them roaming the streets of Orleans.

Two

Willow Sin sat between a newly constructed western saloon and an outdoor barbeque joint. I climbed the steps of the saloon, my boots thumping on the wooden planks. Darkness greeted me when I peered inside. All the stools and even the bar had a coat of dust on them. And the stench of stale beer and sweat hung in the air. I descended the stairs and took in the barbeque place. Picnic tables surrounded a large, steam-powered grill. It looked as if it hadn't been used in a while.

A handwritten sign out front said the place would be closed until further notice.

Yet, Willow Sin sat between the two, lit up like a Christmas tree.

The two-story French inspired building was painted white with pale yellow doors. Magnolias sat in a flower box underneath all the windows. The green awning over the door had a painting of a woman wearing a corset and a man with his jeans so low on his hips you could just make out the line of hair surrounding his manhood.

I pulled open the doors and warm floral-tainted air

rushed out. A fire blazed in the fireplace against the wall. Two old fashioned wood-trimmed couches sat across from one another, with a dark wood coffee table sitting in between. A single chair sat off to the side. Cozy.

A woman sat in the front room with a shotgun resting on her bare thighs. Long red hair pulled up into a bun with a few stray tendrils surrounding her face, she regarded us out of deep blue eyes.

"What's your pleasure, darlin'?" she asked, her red-painted nails tapping lightly on the gun barrel.

"You greet all your customers with that shotgun?" I asked as I eased my hand toward my own, just in case.

The woman shifted her gaze to Pearl, assessing, then smiled, her whole face lighting up with the gesture. "Can't be too careful right now." She stood, giving us an unob-structed view of her black camisole and bare legs. "New Orleans isn't too safe right now. Folks are packing up and leaving." She leaned the gun against the chair and pulled her black, silk robe around her. "Figured I'd get a feel for the person coming through the door before I let them see my girls."

"You do seem to be the only business open," I said.

She nodded. "No amount of danger would ever stop a horny bastard seeking out some company." She studied me for a minute. "Yet, you don't look as if you're pursuing a good time."

It was my turn to smile. I stepped forward. "No. Not looking for a good time. My name's Parasol Daring." I jerked my head toward Pearl. "This is my sister, Pearl."

"Eliza Willow. Most folks call me Ella." She looked at Pearl. "An automaton for a sister. Must be the best kind. My own sister cleaned me out and left when she was eighteen. If I ever see her again, I might put a bullet in her head."

Pearl laughed. "Now you're talking." She extended her arm, showing off my failed attempts to make her look more like me. "My sister covered me in toxic paint when she was seven."

"Why didn't you remove it?" Ella asked.

"It helps when I tell people of the near brush with death at the hands of a deranged seven-year-old."

I shook my head. Pearl loved telling that story.

Ella furrowed her brow. "Wait. Are you the late Bobby Daring's granddaughter?"

I nodded.

She gave me a sympathetic look. "His death must have hit you hard." She reached out and squeezed my hand. "He was a masterful inventor. The first deviser." I smiled at that. He was the first to bring the machines back into the world. "The new man who took over is not half the genius your grandfather was." She shook her head. "Sub-par automatons. It's a good thing other folks have taken up the trade." She frowned. "Although I imagine it's hard seeing your grandfather's work be reduced to trash."

The new man in charge of my grandfather's company had worked for him for twelve years. When my parents were killed by a Soulless One, my grandfather decided he would dedicate his time to finding a way to kill them. So, he sold the company and set out on his mission. His dogged pursuit ended with him becoming the thing he hunted. He'd come to visit me after he changed and told me he'd discovered a way to kill them—then gifted me with the gun and the bullets.

We have been hunting them ever since. It was also the main reason I needed to work now. The money he made from selling his business had all but run out.

But no one knew about our pursuits. Everyone believed he had died, and it needed to stay that way.

"Thank you," I said, infusing just a touch of sadness in my voice. "I miss him every day." That last part was true. After our initial encounter, my grandfather refused to see me. Instead, he sent the bullets I needed via his automaton, George. While he had control over his urges, he still wanted to keep me safe. And the only way to do that was to stay away. Something I hoped, once I killed the First, would change. It was one of the many stories about the Soulless that had been repeated time and time again. The First controlled them all. I was counting on it being true.

"We met a man on the way in," I started, changing the subject. "He told us the sheriff had imposed a curfew. Advised me to take shelter."

"Was he wearing all black?" she asked.

"Yes," Pearl said. "Told Parasol she would fit right in here."

Ella let out a menacing chuckle. "That'd be Clarence McCree. He's still mad as hell about losing the election to ol' Sheriff Longfellow. Looks for every opportunity possible to defy the law." She harrumphed. "He's spent more time in the jail cells than in his own home." Ella paused, then added, "He also has some pretty fucked up ideas about 'a woman's place.' I've had to give him a what for a few times in the past. And since then, he has sent every single young woman to step into town my way. Damn rattlesnake." She scowled.

"I knew he was," Pearl said.

Ella threw her head back and laughed. "Did you call him that?"

"Yes, I did." Pearl lifted her head, pleased.

Ella laughed some more. I let her get it out of her system while I figured out the best way to approach the subject of Clarence's warning. Despite being a rattlesnake and a chauvinist pig, he was out there hunting a Soulless One. Walking headfirst into his own death. Maybe, given Ella's description of him, that might not be so bad.

Damnit, Parasol. It would be bad.

"Well, him and his boys are hunting a Soulless One, so chances are he won't make it through the night," Pearl said as if she were reading my mind again.

Ella rolled her eyes. "Him and his brothers have always bragged about being able to bring down a Soulless One like it's some damn hunting game." She shook her head. "Damn fools. There is no Soulless One in Orleans."

"He said a family was killed out by the bayou. What happened?"

Her eyes went a little distant. She pulled the robe

tighter around her. "Mr. Cummings and his wife and two daughters live out on the bayou." She pulled a tissue from her pocket and wiped at a tear that had slid down her face. "When their neighbor didn't see the girls come out to catch the school boat, he went to check on them." She shivered. "He found them in the living room, torn to pieces." Her mouth thinned as she shook her head. "Those precious girls. Such delightful little ones." Ella looked at me. "Sheriff said the gators had got to them. That would be more likely than a Soulless One. After all, the entire family had been baptized. A Soulless One can't kill the Lord's children. That much we all know."

More lies. More fables. I marveled at the way human beings always found ways to convince themselves they were indestructible. That if they did this, it would protect them from that. It never worked out. And no matter how many times the truth was presented, they were still willing to believe the lie.

"I've heard that before," I said. "It's not true."

She gave me a hard look. "I may be a whore, may have sworn to never set foot in a church again, but I know the power of God. No Soulless One would *dare* harm a saved person," she said with finality.

Despite swearing off church, it was obvious Ella still held on to her religious convictions. "Of course," I said, not wanting to offend her further. I pulled the picture of Covington out of my pocket and extended it to her. "Clarence said this man had come in here. Do you remember him?"

She studied it for a brief second and looked back up at me. "Yeah, that's Lionel Covington's cousin." She tapped her chin. "Frank. Yes, he said his name was Frank. He came through here yesterday. Spent some time with Cherise."

"Cousin?"

She nodded. "Lionel. He comes in here once a week. Lives out on the bayou."

I bit back my anger. No need for her to know that Blankeon had, once again, sent me out on a bounty and withheld vital information that would have made my job easier. If he had told me Covington had a cousin in New Orleans, I would have come here first. Instead of wasting my time and money tracking him all over the damn place.

Which brought up another issue. Why would Blankeon withhold this information? The man who hired him was paying out the ass. Did he want me to fail? Maybe to send someone else? Most likely someone who would accept a lower fee.

Maybe it was the person who was following me.

"Is Cherise here?" I asked finally, filing away my concern for later.

"She's upstairs entertaining. If you care to wait a bit, I can let you talk with her."

"I appreciate that." I shifted. "Your sign out front shows a man and woman," I said, not liking the awkward silence.

She let out a throaty laugh. "I had a few men in here for a while. But they are some moody sons of bitches and didn't take to kindly to me being in charge." She gave me a half smile. "Had to let them go."

The door rattled, drawing all our attention. Pearl moved toward the side window and peered out. She turned and gave me a miniscule shake of her head.

"You two expecting someone?" Ella asked, a note of concern in her voice.

"No," I lied.

If the person following me did show up, I'd deal with them. No need for me to scare Ella. She already looked spooked enough.

"It's late," Ella announced. "Are you two planning on staying the night?"

"Yeah. I understand the other hotel isn't taking guests."

She frowned. "Yeah. Josephine was open for a week before she shut her doors. Said she needed to remodel. But I haven't seen any workmen go in yet." She rubbed her arms as if she had gotten a sudden chill. "I told a few people in town I would let some guests stay if they didn't mind the noise."

I was a light sleeper. But I had no plans on sleeping tonight. I had to hunt. But I also had to wait until everyone had gone to sleep.

"Should be fine," I said.

A muffled grunt filtered down from the upstairs. "Sounds like someone is wrapping it up." Ella tapped her manicured fingers on the counter. "I might have to hurry the other two customers along. The girls usually eat after we close down for the night. If you want, you can join us. It will give you an opportunity to talk with Cherise."

"I appreciate that," I said. "How much for the room?"

Ella pulled a large black ledger from under the counter. "Twenty credits for the room." She winked at me. "I'll throw the meal in for free." She slid the ledger toward me. "I'll need you to sign in."

I scrawled my name on the ledger. My gaze snagged on Covington's name a few entries above mine. "Did Covington have any items with him when he stopped in?" I asked, handing her my last twenty. I would have to stop by the bank in the morning.

She furrowed her brow, thinking. "No. Can't say I noticed him with anything other than a knapsack." She slid the money into her bra. "Although, he did ask where the post service was."

Damn. I should have figured that. He kept making purchases, and I'd assumed he was stashing them somewhere in each of the towns he bought things. Now I just needed to figure out why he was buying relics from the past and who he was shipping them to. Although the former wasn't important and would only serve to satisfy my curiosity, the latter would help with recovering the money he stole. The man who contracted with Blankeon was offering a bonus if I could retrieve his stolen funds. And I really needed that bonus.

Ella stepped around the counter. "The living quarters are down here. The guest rooms are upstairs. Once you're settled, come on down and join us in the dining room."

She pointed to a hallway on the left. "The room should be clean, but if you have any issues, just let me know." She handed me an old-fashioned key.

"Thank you," I said. I took the key and made my way up the stairs.

The long hallway stretched across the entire upper floor, with five rooms on each side of the staircase. An oriental rug covered the soft wood floors. Oil-filled wall sconces lined the hallway, giving off a soft light. A single window sat at the end of the hall with a small cherry, wood table sitting underneath it.

The number on the plastic key ring said she'd put me in room number twelve. Pearl's loud footfalls thumped against the soft wood as we made our way down the hall. Ella's guests probably thought the world was coming to an end.

"Pearl," I admonished.

"Sorry," she said, silencing her steps.

We stopped in front of the door at the end of the hall, near a window. I glanced out and was treated to a view of the restaurant's brick wall. I surveyed the space between and noted the access point from the rear. If anyone did traverse through there, it would be a tight squeeze. Pearl turned on her scan and ran it the entire length of the room.

"All clear," she announced. I unlocked and opened the door. The same floral scent hung heavy in the air, mixed in with a faint smell of old sex.

A four-poster bed lay in the center of the room with a

white net secured around it. Black straps were attached to the sides of the bed. Two nightstands sat on either side, with lamps and a silver antique clock on top. A single chair sat up against the wall near the window. Simple. But then again, most people who visited Willow Sin weren't looking to stay the night.

Gauzy white curtains covered the single window in the room. I walked over and glanced out of it. Dark water deposits with patches of land stretched out for miles. A few homes were scattered around. A short brick wall kept the water from seeping into town.

The person following me had to show themselves at some point. I wondered if they would get the same warning I got. Or if they would end up coming face to face with the Soulless One. If they did, it would solve one of my problems. Although it wouldn't tell me who had sent them to track me in the first place. I was still leaning toward Blankeon. And now that I knew the man had sent me out blind, I had to wonder about his intentions.

A long moan sounded from next door, and Pearl turned toward the wall. "Looks like they're finishing up." She chuckled. "Well, at least he has. Didn't hear a peep out of the woman."

I laughed, set my bags on the bed, and went into the adjoining bathroom. A little on the smallish side with a sink, toilet, and showerhead over a drain in the floor. The walls were done in yellow like the trim on the outside, with flower designs drawn onto the paint. The faint scent of mildew hung in the air, mixing with the floral scent. I was beginning to think Ella used the flowers to hide the other pungent scents that were often found around large bodies of free-standing water.

After using the restroom and washing my hands and face, I went back out into the bedroom and found Pearl staring out the window. "I sent word to George that we need more ammunition," she said, waving to the open case on my bed. She had loaded my gun and pulled out my fighting leathers. "He asked if we were okay. Said him and grandpa were in Mississippi tracking a group of Soulless Ones."

A pang of sadness overcame me. He was so close. I missed my grandpa. It would be nothing to make an excuse to go find him. Help him with his pursuit. But I had to respect his wishes. "I hope you said hello for me."

She nodded, still not looking at me. She missed him too.

I stared down at the items on the bed, pushing thoughts of my grandpa out of my head. "I don't like this," I said. "Something is off about this bounty. This town."

Pearl turned and faced me. "You think it's a setup?"

I gave her a skeptical look. "I don't know, Pearl. Why would Covington come here? Why wouldn't Blankeon tell me about his cousin. And the Soulless One. That can't be a coincidence."

We both stared at each other, and I could tell the moment she came to the same conclusion as I did. "Someone knows," we said in unison.

"There's no way!" Pearl paced around the room, not bothering to silence her footsteps. "We're so careful."

I walked over and put a hand on her arm. "We will handle it," I whispered, encouraging her to quiet down. If someone found out about me hunting the Soulless, they would want to know how I was able to kill them. Which would lead back to my grandfather being a Soulless One. The one supplying me with the means to kill them. I didn't doubt they would use me to get to him and once they had him under their control, they'd use his weapon for money and power.

Not to mention the other Soulless would learn he was the one killing his own kind. If the government didn't get him, the Soulless would. I couldn't let that happen.

"I'm going out to take care of the man following us. You can eat and make nice with the women," she said, infusing her voice with authority. I tried not to laugh. Her bossiness was another quirk that had to have come from my grandfather's programming.

"No. We stick together." I gave her a stern look. "Always."

"I can't be killed, Parasol. But you can."

"True. But you can be taken. All they have to do is get close enough to shut your main power down. If that happens, I will scorch this earth looking for you. Do you want me to have to go through that?"

She smiled. "Might be nice to see you riding in on Betsy. Her nostrils flaring fire and your guns blazing like some long-forgotten heroine from the Wild West."

I shook my head. "You, dear sister, have issues."

"I was programed this way." She leaned in. "What's your excuse?"

"Keep it up, and I'll paint the other arm."

"You wouldn't dare," she said, narrowing her eyes. A smile crept across her face, and I breathed a sigh of relief. I didn't need her going out there killing folks. We needed to be smart about this. I had no proof Blankeon had set me up. So, I would do my job until I knew for sure. But once I found out whether that bastard had taken a hit out on me, I'd put a bullet in his brain. Knowing there was a threat in town, I secured my elk-handled knife around my thigh just in case.

Five women were sitting around a large table when we entered the dining room. I took in the space, noting the open French doors directly behind them. It was a habit of mine. Always cataloging the exits just in case, I had to make a hasty retreat.

If I had to guess, I'd say the room used to be a parlor. Four round tables took up most of the space. The walls were painted the same yellow as the front room, and a door led to the kitchen. Delicious smells of bacon and eggs wafted out making my mouth water. Reminding me I hadn't eaten since morning.

Steam filled the room, and I turned to the chrome-coated coffee maker sitting on a long table near the door.

Aquagold sat in a drum on the side of the table, feeding into a cylindrical tube connected to a cog. It was the first model I'd seen that didn't make a shit ton of noise.

"Ella just got that last week," one of the girls offered. "She loves showing it off."

"How did she get the Aquagold?" I asked, curious.

When Mother Nature had cleansed the planet, she'd cut off access to gas and oil. Human beings had to rely on fire once again. Until a group of women calling themselves, The Kai found deposits of the oil like substance laced with gold on the old Native American reservations. It took only a cup full of the new element to power steam engines and lamps. Pearl and Betsy used the material as well. As far as I knew, only the western parts of the country had access to it. It was where my grandpa had acquired his stash of the expensive substance.

The kitchen door swung open, and Ella walked in carrying a platter of bacon, eggs, bread, and fruit in one hand and her shotgun in the other. "Have a regular that works out west. On his last visit, he paid me with the stuff," she said with a wink. "Figured the Aquagold should last until he stops in again. Now, please sit. Meet my girls."

I walked over and took a seat facing the French doors. I never sat with my back to the door. Too easy to get killed that way.

"Ladies, this is Parasol Daring and her sister, Pearl." Ella set the platter on the table and rested her shotgun on the floor next to her chair.

They smiled at us.

"I'm thinking of getting myself an automaton," a dark-skinned woman said as she scooped food onto her plate. "Might help me handle some of the rough ones."

Ella gave her a pointed look. "We talked about this. Someone gets rough, you come get me, Linda."

Linda stared at her. "Even after last time?"

The other girls stopped eating and clasped each other's arms as if reassuring themselves that they were okay. The love and concern for one another was written all over their faces.

Ella's lips thinned and she lifted her chin. "Won't happen again," she all but gritted out. She patted the shotgun leaning against her chair.

Finally, Linda nodded and took a bite of her bacon.

Ella sighed. "My girls say what does and does not go down when they take a man upstairs. We've had a few come in here recently who didn't understand that. When the last one managed to overpower me, I bought a gun. Now, they think twice about their behavior." She dipped her head toward a young woman with short black hair and deep chestnut eyes. "Cherise, Parasol wants to know about Frank Covington." Ella settled back with a cup of coffee, keeping her eyes on Cherise.

She was damn protective of her girls. I admired her. It had to be hard maintaining control in her line of work.

"Hi," I said, offering her a smile.

She returned the smile. Cherise looked to be in her early twenties. She still had that bright, wide-eyed look in her eyes about life that time would soon dim to a mere spark.

"Yeah. I spent a few hours with him." She shrugged and picked up her toast. "He was okay. Better than most who come in here who don't bathe on a regular basis." The rest of the girls murmured consent. I kept the look of disgust off my face and waited for her to continue.

Cherise spread grape jam over her bread, her eyes distant as if she were recalling something. "I thought it was funny that he kept talking about the relics he was buying and how the information in them was going to change the world." She took a bite of her toast and closed her eyes, savoring it. "Like the past could change our future or something," she said after she finished chewing.

I, too, was more than a little curious as to why he felt some old relics would change the world. Pearl set a cup of coffee in front of me, and I nodded my thanks. "Did he give you any details on how?" I asked after taking a sip. The coffee was pretty damn good. Not watered down like most places I'd been to. It still held onto its rich body and flavor. Even the dark, nutty aroma was tantalizing.

She wrinkled her nose. "No. He just kept repeating it. When I told him I had to get back downstairs, he fucked me again, gave me a big tip, and left."

"Did he mention anything about his cousin? Tell you he was going to stay with him?"

"I've spent some time with Lionel," one of the girls said. "Although, he hasn't been in this week yet."

"Is that unusual?" I asked, directing my question to Ella, since the girl who said it had resumed eating.

She shook her head. "Not too much. He's gone a week or two without company in the past. Could be he wants to spend time with his cousin."

"To answer your question," Cherise said, "no, he didn't say if he was staying with Lionel. Only said his cousin told him to stop in."

"I'll need directions to Lionel's house," I said, leaning back.

Ella studied me. "What kind of trouble is Frank in?"

Before I could answer, a noise out front drew our attention. Ella jumped up and grabbed her shotgun. The girls stood. Ella shook her head. "You all stay here," she told them. She dipped her gun barrel toward the French doors. "Lock the doors and don't come out unless I call for you."

They nodded, and one of the girls rushed over and pulled the doors closed.

I had a moment of indecision before Pearl and I rushed out to join her.

I yanked my knife from its sheath—cursing myself for not bringing my gun down with me instead.

The three of us arrived in the front room at the same time.

Warm, damp air slapped me in the face along with the sickly scent of copper and brine.

A man wearing dark jeans and a dark blue shirt stood in the doorway, with a leather sack secured over his shoulder. Strands of his long black hair lay plastered to his face. His bright hazel eyes locked with mine, and he smiled, letting go of the bloody man he held by the collar.

Ella cocked her gun and pointed at the man. He stared at her with a smile on his face. "You know this man, Parasol?" she asked, gritting the words out.

"Jackson Pureifoy," I said, my heart ramming in my chest.

She lowered the gun.

"Parasol." Jackson looked over my shoulder. "Pearl." He dipped his head toward the mangled man at his feet. "I believe this one might have lost his soul."

"Well, shit," Pearl said.

Looked like Orleans did have a Soulless One roaming the streets after all.

# THREE

What was left of Clarence McCree lay crumpled at Jackson's feet. A coppery scent wafted through the air, competing with all the other smells pushing their way inside the front door. His once pristine black trench coat had been torn to shreds. His neck and stomach had been ripped open, exposing the organs underneath.

I walked over and knelt in front of Clarence. "Where'd you find him, Jackson?"

He thumbed over his shoulder. "Out in the middle of the road. Near that hotel."

Josephine's Place.

"Why bring him here?" I asked.

"Only place with the lights on, darlin'."

I turned away from that smile and studied Clarence's neck. Two fang marks had pierced his carotid artery leaving behind a mangled mess. Blood had dried on his skin making it look as if he had a rash on his neck. All the carnage from a Soulless One attack gave the illusion that they drank their victim's blood.

It wasn't true.

It was the madness and pain the Soulless Ones suffered. The pain they wanted their victims to experience as well. And once their prey died, they consumed the souls as they departed the body. All twenty-one grams. And once ingested, the soul would degrade. Similar to the way a transplanted organ behaved when the body rejected it. Forcing the Soulless to find another soul—or souls—to ease their endless suffering.

"Did you see his brothers?" I asked, standing. Didn't make sense for Jackson to only find Clarence if he had planned to go hunting for the Soulless One with his brothers. Unless they had gotten away.

Jackson studied me, his eyes roaming over my entire body. I used to love those looks. Especially when we lay in bed together. But now, I couldn't stand the sight of him.

I narrowed my eyes, waiting for him to respond.

"Is that all you have to say?" he asked, his tone level.

Pearl harrumphed. "Jackass," she mumbled.

"I should call the sheriff," Ella said, making her way around the counter.

"Answer the question," I gritted out.

He shook his head and scrubbed his hand down his face. "I just found him, with his gun still clutched in his hand." He pulled Clarence's gun from his waistband and handed it to me. "All the rounds are still in it. Silver."

I'd tried to warn the idiot. Well, maybe not directly, but I did try and instill some doubt. And where were his damn brothers?

"Sheriff said he'd be here in a minute and everyone

should wait." Ella pulled in a breath as if she were trying to compose herself. "Maybe I should make some more coffee." She stood there for a minute, looking around. "I knew . . ."

Pearl went around the counter and pulled her into a hug. "There, now. It's always hard seeing death the first time."

Ella pulled away. "Thank you, Pearl. No. I'm not . . ." She flapped her hand in Clarence's direction. "I've seen a dead body before. Just never someone I knew." She gave a humorless laugh. "Not that I was particularly fond of Clarence. The man was a mean bastard. I sadly learned that *after* I'd slept with him. Made him pay extra for the meanness. But still. Oh, I'm rattling on. I'll go make that coffee." She walked out the room, and we all stood there staring after her.

"I can't believe she slept with that rattlesnake," Pearl said. She turned and glowered at Jackson. "So, I suppose you're the one been following us? *'Fuck off'* not working for you? You need more instructions on how to stay away?"

"I missed you, too, Pearl." He smiled, and my insides flipped. "Yeah. Been following you since Crest City. Saw you showing Covington's picture around thought I might lend a hand."

"Oh, I see. You still think Parasol is some weak-willed woman, unable to handle herself. And you're going to ride in here on your white horse—"

"Horse is black, Pearl. You know that." His mouth twitched. He was enjoying this.

Pearl stomped over and stood next to me. The floorboards groaned. "Listen here, Mr. Jackson Pureifoy. I am two seconds away from wrenching your manhood off and shoving it—"

I put my hand on Pearl. "It's all right, Pearl. I can handle him."

She glared at him, eyes going red. Like she was going to fry him alive. "Fine. I will make myself useful." She glanced down at Clarence. "Rattlesnake," she spat then moved behind the counter.

"Thank you," I said, not taking my eyes off Jackson. Smug bastard was way too amused for my comfort.

I grabbed Jackson's arm and steered him toward the corner of the room. Ella had returned with the coffee. She handed a cup to Jackson, and he winked at her. She smiled, pulling her robe closed, and moved away.

I rounded on him. "Why are you really following me?" I asked in a harsh whisper.

Despite what Pearl said, I knew Jackson didn't think of me as a weak-willed woman. He and I would never have spent time together if I had been. He'd once told me that when his mother tried to marry him off to some corset-wearing, pampered debutant, he'd run away from home. I'd met him two years ago on a job. I'd just finished getting paid when Jackson stormed in and accused me of stealing his bounty. Blankeon, believing I couldn't complete the job, had decided to hire backup. We yelled at each other for an hour, then got a room and fucked till the sun came up. It was the best sex I'd ever had.

And I foolishly made the mistake of telling him that.

"Wanted to see you," he said finally. "Figured we could . . . " He trailed off and took a sip of his coffee. I glared at him. "Damn, Parasol. Don't know what I figured, but I knew I wanted to see you."

"Like my sister asked, was '*fuck off*' not clear enough for you?"

The door opened. Jackson pulled his gun from his holster, and I raised Clarence's and pointed it at the door. I should have sent Pearl to get my gun. I hated using someone else's. Especially a dead man's.

A tall man walked in wearing a disheveled dark blue coat and half button white shirt with gold badge clipped to his blue jeans. A dark gray Stetson rested on his head. Behind him, a much shorter man came in looking more pristine in his pale blue button-down shirt and dark jeans. His badge was pinned to his shirt pocket.

An automaton whirred in after them.

The first man—who I assumed was the sheriff—took in our guns, Clarence, and Ella's bare legs before settling his gaze back on Clarence. "Damn fool," he said, then removed his hat and stood silent for a moment. After a short while, he put his hat back on and looked at us. "You two can lower your weapons now. Unless you want to spend some time in our jail." He gave us a hard look.

Almost daring us to keep our guns trained on him. I had to admit, I was tempted. Something about him rubbed me the wrong way.

Jackson lowered his gun and looked at me. After a brief hesitation, I gave him Clarence's gun. Didn't matter. It wasn't mine to begin with and I still had my knife. Pearl stomped into the room and stood next to me.

"Now," the man said, sparing Pearl a brief glance. "Who found the body?"

Jackson moved around me. "I did," he said. "He was near Josephine's place." He extended the gun to the sheriff. "Found this still in his hands."

He took it from Jackson and gave it to the man behind him. "Sheriff Longfellow," he said. "This is my deputy, Lance Whitman." He gave Jackson a questioning look. "Want to tell me why you tampered with the evidence?"

"Jackson Pureifoy," Jackson said instead of answering. "I work as a Marshal out of South California." He pulled a badge from his back pocket. "Just sworn in two weeks ago."

My eyes rounded. The Jackson I knew worked so far outside of the law that they might as well be on different planets. Why the hell would he join the Marshal Service? And why the hell would they hire him?

The sheriff narrowed his eyes. "Marshall service doesn't have jurisdiction in my town." the sheriff said.

Jackson gave me a brief glance, then pulled a rolled-up file out of his pocket. "This here says I do." He handed the sheriff the file. The man gave it a cursory glance, still wearing a look of anger on his face. "I'm here for Frank Covington."

"The hell you are," Pearl yelled.

I gave her a look, silencing her. Wanted to see me, my ass. The bastard was trying to take in my bounty. And what would the Marshal Service want with Covington anyway?

Sheriff Longfellow turned his gaze to me. "And you?"

"Parasol Daring. I'm a bounty hunter. *Also* looking for Frank Covington." I crossed my arms over my chest.

"Are you related to the late Bobby Daring?" he asked, eyeing Pearl again with a more critical eye.

"Yes." I pulled my credentials out of my back pocket and handed them to him.

He took my paperwork and looked it over. "Looks like the two of you have some problems to sort out." He handed me back my paperwork and looked over at the automaton unit whirring in place.

It wasn't one of my grandfather's designs. His old protégé didn't like the idea of automatons looking human. Said it was unnatural. The first thing he did when he took over was redesign them, giving them a more robotic look with round parts, spindly arms and legs, wheels for movement, and featureless heads. I hated them. Like Ella said, all my grandfather's hard work, gone.

"I'm not real happy about you all disturbing the scene." The sheriff sighed. "Unit 34, send word to the coroner and scan the scene here and outside."

An electronic whine pierced the air. "I have notified the corner. Case number?" it asked.

Sheriff Longfellow pulled a notebook from his pocket, then said, "SM-4567A. Authorized."

"Logging, SM-4567A. Authorized by Sheriff Reginald Longfellow of the New Orleans Police Department." The unit scanned Clarence McCree first. "Identification confirmed. Clarence McCree. Citizen. Builder. Deceased. Scene scan to commence in 30 seconds. All unauthorized personnel must leave the immediate area."

Sheriff Longfellow turned to Ella. "We need to move to a different room."

She nodded. "We can wait in the dining room."

"Deputy. I need you to secure the scene out front."

His deputy nodded and stepped outside. The rest of us followed Ella down the short hallway and into the dining room. The girls were gone—leaving half-eaten food behind. The sheriff glanced at the food and raised an eyebrow. "You have guests?" he asked, a note of anger lacing his tone.

Ella bristled. "Just my girls, Ms. Daring, and her sister Pearl."

The sheriff turned to me. "Where's your sister?"

"I'm right here," Pearl said.

The sheriff studied her for a minute, his eyes dancing with humor. I prayed he didn't say anything. If he did, I doubt I could keep Pearl off him. He walked over to the coffee maker and fixed himself a cup. After taking a long sip, he took off his hat and set it on the table, then turned his gaze to encompass me and Jackson. "So. Who wants to start?" he asked.

I pulled a chair out and sat down heavily. "I took the bounty on Covington last Tuesday. I was hired by Tony Blankeon to bring him in dead or alive. I tracked him across two cities before arriving here," I said, sitting back. I wasn't going to give him any more information than necessary. He wasn't paying my fees. I turned to Jackson. He had the nerve to give me a pitying look.

Jackson leaned against the wall and kept his eyes on me. "Marshal Service sent me out to bring him in. Seems Covington has some information on a wanted man, and we wanted to secure his cooperation." He turned to look at Sheriff Longfellow. "The rest is classified."

"Classified?" Sheriff Longfellow nodded, looking deep in thought. "Well, marshal, looks like you're going to have to check with the powers that be on un-classifying it. We've got a murder on our hands, and it seems the common denominator here is the two of you and Frank Covington."

We all stared at him. That was a giant leap. One I was sure he didn't believe himself. Just like his telling the locals that gators had killed Mr. Cummings and his family. What was the man playing at?

"Clarence claimed a family was killed the other night by a Soulless One," I accused. "When I came into town, he told me him and his boys were hunting it."

Sheriff Longfellow gave me a hard look. I gave him one right back.

The crime unit whirred into the dining room. "The scene has been processed. The body has been removed," it announced. That was quick.

Sheriff Longfellow finished his coffee and set the mug on the table. "Ms. Willow. Be sure and make these two comfortable." He looked at us. "Come to the station in the morning. We'll see about picking up Frank Covington, and you two can decide who will bring him in to your prospective employers. Once you have him in custody, I trust you won't need to stay any longer in our city." The way he said it, sounded as if he knew exactly where Covington was.

I stood up. "If you know where he is, I can take him in now."

Sheriff turned, dismissing me. "I'm going to keep a man downstairs if that's all right with you, Ms. Willow."

She bristled but nodded her consent.

"Good." He looked down at her legs. "Nice seeing you, as always." He walked out without another word.

"Nice fella," Jackson said. "Also completely off base."

Ella flipped off the door the sheriff had walked out of and turned to Jackson. "I suppose I should get you a room as well." She looked at me, her mouth turning up into a smile. "Unless you two are sharing."

I narrowed my eyes. "No," we both said in unison.

She shrugged and walked out of the room. After a brief pause, we followed her.

Ella decided to give Jackson the room next to mine. I smiled, knowing she might not have had time to clean it.

Despite that knowledge, I was still a little upset that she was obviously trying to play matchmaker. Then again, even a blind man could see the sexual tension between us.

Before going into his room, Jackson turned to me. "Sorry I didn't tell you about the Marshal Service when I last saw you."

"I thought you were sworn in two weeks ago," I said, an accusatory note in my voice.

He sighed. "I've been training with them for a year."

I scoffed. "They let any old trash in, huh?" I tried to cover my wince. Even to me, that sounded too harsh. There was nothing wrong with Jackson per se. We just had bad timing, and we both were too damn stubborn for our own good. Unwilling to give even an inch.

He covered his own hurt with a forced smile. "I just thought I would apologize." He turned to leave, and I grabbed his arm.

"Wait." I sucked in a deep breath. "You didn't deserve that." I stared up at him. "I'm happy for you."

He leaned in. "How happy?"

I put my hand on his chest. "Don't push it." I turned and stared down the hall. "What do you make of the sheriff?" I asked after a short pause.

"Seems like he doesn't want us in his city."

"Yeah. And posting a man downstairs almost guarantees that we won't go out and investigate what's going on. Maybe I shouldn't have told him what Clarence said."

"Wouldn't have mattered. Whatever that man has

going on, he is willing to shut down an entire town to do it. We'll collect Clarence in the morning and leave."

I started to protest, but that would mean admitting I had plans to go after the Soulless One. Jackson didn't know I could kill them, and I wanted to keep it that way.

"Keep your gun close," I said.

He winked at me. "I always do, darlin'."

We stood there staring at each other for a moment. The air charged between us. It would have been so easy to slip back into our familiar pattern. Hell, we were in the right place for it. But I had to keep my distance. Especially now that Jackson was working for the government.

"Care to tell me who the Marshals have their eye on?" I asked, softening my tone.

He laughed. "You know I'm not that easy, darlin'." He leaned in again. "But maybe if you work on it, I might let a clue or two loose."

I backed up. "Goodnight, Jackson."

He stared at me a moment more, then said, "Night, darlin'. Try not to miss me too much." He glanced behind me. "Night, Pearl. Try not to sneak in my room and relieve me of my manhood."

"You best sleep with one eye open," she said.

He laughed and went to his room.

I washed up in the adjoining bathroom and put on a fresh pair of jeans. Once dressed, I picked up my special-made revolver and loaded the remaining five silver bullets into one barrel, the soul capsules in the other. I wasn't going to take any chances. I gave the bed a long sad look, then settled into a chair in the middle of the floor.

"Get some sleep, Parasol," Pearl said. "I can stop anything that would dare come through the door."

She could. But if a Soulless One did come through the door, I needed to be alert and ready. I couldn't let Pearl deal with it on her own.

"I'm fine, Pearl."

Pearl sighed and brought over a small vial of red-gold serum. "You'll need this," she said.

I took the bottle from her and, after a brief hesitation, downed the contents. The concoction was made from Aquagold and a drop of my grandfather's blood. It would give me added sight and strength to fight the Soulless One.

It raced through my system, giving off a scorching heat. I swallowed, pushing down the fiery bile that rose in my throat, and let the concoction work its way through my system. My vision changed, making every detail in the room pulse.

Another myth about Soulless Ones was that they looked dead. That their waxy complexion and washed-out eyes would allow someone to pick them out in a crowd. Of course, it wasn't true. They looked just like anyone else.

And unless one could see the stolen soul inside of them, they wouldn't know they were dealing with a Soulless One until it was too late.

Thanks to the concoction, I could see.

I leaned back in my chair and rested my gun on my thigh prepared to wait out the night.

FOUR

Someone knocked on my door, and I bolted up out of the chair. I had fallen asleep. Fuck. I wiped the sleep from my eyes and glanced at the clock on the nightstand. Seven in the morning. I turned and scowled at Pearl. "You let me fall asleep," I accused.

She crossed her arms and met my gaze with a scowl of her own. "You needed the rest."

I shook my head and glared at the door. I doubted Ella would come up and disturb me this early in the morning. That left only one other person. Jackson. I didn't have the patience to deal with him this morning. Sadly, there was nothing I could do about it. We had to settle the issue of who got to take Covington in. It might come to blows. I smiled at the thought, then remembered the last time we went at it and ended up in bed. I sighed and walked to the door.

I was not going to sleep with Jackson Pureifoy.

I pulled open the door, and Jackson's familiar leather and sandalwood scent slapped me in the face and threatened to make a liar out of me. He'd showered. His dark curly hair hung loose around his head, bringing back memories of me threading my fingers through it while Jackson took his time with me. He never shaved. Always had a light dusting of hair surrounding his sensual mouth. Black jeans rode low on his hips, hugging his powerful thighs.

"Did you want me to turn around so you can inspect the back, darlin'?" he asked and winked.

Oh, that did it. "Why are you knocking at my door so damn early in the morning?" I asked through my teeth.

He took in my disheveled clothes and hair. "Hard night?"

"Fuck you."

"You wish."

I glared at him while I suppressed the sudden tightening in my stomach at the thought of me and Jackson stretched out on the bed. No, wasn't going to go there again.

He glanced behind me. "Pearl," he said, smiling.

"Jackass," she said, coming to stand next to me.

"It's Jackson," he said.

"That's what I said, Jackass."

I shifted closer. If I didn't stop this, he and Pearl would go at it all day. Jackson adored Pearl and really got a kick out of her needling him. Pearl thought he was a scoundrel and had offered on more than one occasion to relieve him of his manhood. Our on-again, off-again relationship was confusing to her. So instead of warming to him when we were on again, she decided needling him all the time was safer.

"You didn't answer my question, *Jackson*. What are you doing at my door so early in the morning?"

He leaned against the doorframe and stared down at me. "Figured we'd head to the sheriff's office together."

I figured as much too. But I still didn't like the early intrusion. I hadn't had any coffee. Not to mention my back was killing me from sitting in the chair all damn night.

"You plan on trying to steal my bounty? Because that will not end well for you. I'm bringing him in, so don't get in my damn way."

"Never said I would. I'd just have to remove him from Blankeon's care after you collect your fee."

He was actually going to let me take Covington to Blankeon. "Why would you do that?"

His face softened, and he stared down at me for a minute. "Figured I owed you," he said finally. "I also figured we could travel together." The hope in his eyes gave me pause. What was Jackson getting at?

"Why do you want to work with me?" I asked. "And what makes you think I'm bringing him in alive?"

"Well." He put his hat on. "I get the impression the sheriff will have the man cuffed and ready to go when we get there. There's no need for you to shoot him." He winked and gave me one of his disarming smiles. Damn this man got under my skin.

I pushed farther into his space. "If you are thinking

about double-crossing me, Covington won't be the only one I put a bullet in."

He leaned in, stealing all the air in the room. "Is that a threat, darlin'?"

I swallowed, licking my lips. He tracked the movement with his eyes. I needed to shut this down now. "Move out of my way, Jackson."

He didn't move.

Finally, I moved away and started gathering my things, aware of his eyes tracking me the entire time and Pearl's gaze fixed on him, waiting. I'd call it a standoff, but we all knew we wouldn't do anything. There was too much love between us. Don't get me wrong, there was hate, too. But underneath all our bickering, we had something. We just weren't in a place to make something of it.

I went into the bathroom to wash my face, and Pearl joined me.

"What is up with him?" she asked, still staring at the open door.

I shook my head. "I don't know, Pearl. I don't know." And I didn't have the time to try and figure it out. I had other things to worry about. Like why the sheriff would hand Covington over and tell us to leave his town. And how I was going to engineer it so I didn't have to leave. Giving me the opportunity to hunt down the Soulless One.

Ella had set up a breakfast buffet in the eating area. Steam rose from her coffee machine as the gears ground, brewing the coffee. I grabbed a cup to help take the edge off my tiredness, along with a muffin to appease my hunger, and walked out into the swampy air.

Storm clouds had settled over the town. The warm air lay on my skin like a wet, warm blanket. I swatted a mosquito away and went into the community barn to retrieve Betsy. I was acutely aware of Jackson behind me but chose to ignore his presence. A man stood in the middle of the room, brushing a gray horse. He turned when we walked in. No more than five foot eleven, the man wore dirty coveralls and a hat that had seen better days. He chewed on a piece of straw as he continued to watch me.

"Mr. Stevens?" I asked by way of greeting.

He nodded, then dipped his head toward the back. "That your horse?"

"Yes," I said. "I need to stop by the bank this morning to get you your fee."

He shook his head. "It's all right. Sheriff settled the bill for you and the other fella this mornin'." He stopped brushing the horse and pulled the straw from his mouth. "Something's not quite right with your horse. Tried to feed her this morning, but she didn't eat. Then wouldn't let me brush her."

"She's temperamental. And only eats apples," I said in an apologetic tone. Few people knew that Betsy was a mishmash of mechanical and horse parts, and I wanted to keep it that way. "Why would the sheriff pay our bill?" I asked. Jackson walked over to the stall next to Betsy and pulled his horse out. A black Friesian he named Ol' Nick due to his gentle nature. I smiled at the sight of the beautiful horse. He clopped over and sniffed at my bag. I pulled out an apple and rubbed his neck. If there was anything I missed about seeing Jackson, it would be his horse, Nick. The gentlest creature I had ever met. He never got spooked by Betsy's strangeness.

Mr. Stevens scratched the scruff on his chin. "He's making sure everyone gets out of town before nightfall." A sad look overcame him. "More people were killed last night. Including Clarence McCree." He shook his head. "Man was a snake through and through, but he didn't deserve what happened to him."

I cursed inwardly. I should have found a way to slip out last night and hunt down the Soulless One. Now, more people were dead.

"What did the sheriff say happened?" Jackson asked before I could.

Mr. Stevens looked up at him. "Said it was a gun accident. One of his brothers confessed to shooting him. Sad state of affairs." He turned away and resumed brushing the horse.

I started to tell him the sheriff was lying, but Jackson put his hand on my arm and gave a minuscule shake of his head. Why was the sheriff lying to everyone?

After retrieving Betsy, I walked out of the stall. The

space between my shoulder blades started to itch, I turned and found Mr. Stevens watching us.

Despite the sheriff paying the bill for me lodging Betsy, I still needed to get money out for the journey back. When I stopped in front of the bank, I was greeted by a sign that said the bank was temporarily closed. I turned and looked at Pearl. "Something is really off here."

Jackson stood in the middle of the road, scanning the buildings one by one. "It's like they shut the whole town down," he said, his voice taking on a note of concern. He put his hand on his gun and turned to me. "Have Pearl watch the horses while we retrieve Covington."

I would have balked at his orders, but I had been about to suggest the same thing. Betsy could take care of herself and even look out for Jackson's horse. But in case we ran into trouble and had to fight our way out, I needed our exit clear.

Pearl, for once, didn't scowl at Jackson, and after a quick goodbye, Jackson and I headed down the cobble-stone path toward the sheriff's office. We turned down the first side street and were deposited on a path lined with water.

Only a few businesses sat on the street. The New Orleans Police Department rested at the end. The building rose up above all the rest, sitting on large brick blocks. Large cypress trees covered in Spanish moss surrounded the small building, their ghostly fingers trailing in the water deposits along the ground. A steam-powered generator sat on a platform next to the station, pumping steam into the air. The entire area smelled like rotted wood and dead things.

We climbed the five wooden steps and walked into the hot building. Ceiling fans whirred overhead, pushing the damp heat around the room. The smell of stale coffee and tobacco overpowered the scents from outside, and I pinched my nose to keep from sneezing.

Five officers and two automatons made up the entire police force. The officers' desks rested in a zig zag line facing the front door. The automatons sat in the corner of the room with their glassy eyes trained on the front door. Directly behind them were two doors. One leading to jail cells, the other to the sheriff's office. Sheriff Longfellow stepped out through the second door, gave us a once over, and walked to the cells. A short while later, he came out with Frank Covington in tow. The man wore a look of resolve on his face. Like he had given up and was resigned to his fate.

Sheriff Longfellow stopped in front of us and undid Frank's cuffs. "I trust you two slept all right," he said, not looking at us. "Ella said she put out breakfast. And this one has already been fed." He finally looked up. "Hope you sorted out which of you get to take him in. Either way, since you have no other business in town, I trust you'll be on your way."

"And you conveniently paid for our horses as well," I

said, my voice flat. "If I didn't know any better, I'd say you were rushing us out of town."

He nodded. "We've had some trouble, and I'd prefer strangers steer clear at the moment."

"You told Mr. Stevens that Clay's brother shot him," Jackson said, giving him a hard look. "What kind of gun rips a man's neck and stomach out?"

We both had yet to take hold of Covington. Because when we did, we'd have no reason to stay behind. And I was more than a little concerned about why he was rushing us along. Especially since we both knew a Soulless One was committing the crimes. I started to say as much but held my tongue. I'd let Jackson work his way around to it.

"Not your concern," the sheriff said, voice hard.

Jackson opened his mouth to respond, then stopped and looked over at me. "Darlin'?"

"There is a Soulless One roaming the streets of Orleans, and you and I both know this," I said, glaring at the sheriff. "Now why would you want to lie to the people you are supposed to be protecting?"

The sheriff got in my face, his eyes blazing with anger. "Like I told your *friend* here. It. Is. Not. Your. Concern. Now." He shoved Covington at me. I barely managed to keep from falling. "Get the hell out of my town. If you're here when the sun goes down, I will put you in a cell and forget you're there."

I pushed Covington away and stepped into the sheriff's space. His eyes widened. Shocked. Cold crept into my voice. I didn't tolerate anyone disrespecting me. Not even a lawman who, from what I could see, was either corrupt or so far out of his depth, he couldn't find his way back if someone led him to it. "Is it fear?" I asked, voice soft. "Or stupidity that you have stenciled on the blindfold you've decided to wear?"

He reached for me, and I smiled, waiting for him to take it to the next level. If he put me in his cell, Pearl would break me out. And soon after, I'd put my boot in his back.

But, sadly, before the sheriff could say anything, Jackson grabbed my arm and pulled me away. "Thank you for your time," he said, grabbing Covington with his other hand and pulling us both out of the station.

As soon as we stepped outside, I turned to Jackson. "Why did you stop me?"

Jackson's eyes narrowed. "Because you were two seconds away from being locked up." He glanced inside the police station. "Let's get going." He rounded on Covington. "On behalf of the California Marshal Service, I'm placing you under arrest." The man whimpered. "You can walk on your own or I can drag you. Which do you prefer?"

"I knew you were going to double cross me," I said before Covington could respond.

Jackson gave me a look. One that I knew all too well. He didn't trust the situation we were in. I looked back into the station. All the officers were standing, watching us. Indecision warred inside of me. I had lost my temper in there. I could blame lack of sleep, but I knew it was more than that. The sheriff's behavior had rubbed me the wrong way.

I didn't know all the people in this town. Had no real ties to anyone but my grandfather and Pearl and, on occasion, Jackson. But that didn't stop me from being concerned about others' wellbeing. Especially when I knew I could do something to help. I had entertained, briefly, not getting involved. But even then, I knew I would. I had promised my grandfather I would keep our secret. But I'd also promised myself I would kill every last Soulless One I came across.

And if that meant defying the useless sheriff, and losing the reward I so desperately needed, so be it.

I looked at Jackson. He was waiting for me to make a decision.

Finally, I said, "We can deal with this later."

Jackson nodded and started down the stairs. Covington didn't hesitate to follow. And after giving the sheriff one last look, I walked down the stairs too.

When we were well out of earshot, Covington turned to me. "I need you to let me go."

"Not going to happen," I said.

He sighed and turned away. "I will go willingly. But first, I need to save my cousin."

"From what?" I asked.

"The Soulless Ones."

FIVE

Pearl was waiting by the horses when we returned. She'd removed my riding blanket and secured my transport saddle that had straps with a locking mechanism on it. I'd had the saddle made when I first started bounty hunting. I refused to get another horse to bring in my bounties. Another horse meant more money spent on boarding and feeding, and I didn't want to waste my funds on anything outside of paying for my living expenses. Life on the road was hard, and not every town had a bank, so I had to be frugal where money was concerned.

I'd been thinking about what Covington said when we left the police department. As long as I'd been hunting them, no one else had referred to the Soulless Ones in the plural form. It was always 'a Soulless One.' But Covington had said Soulless *Ones*. Which meant there was more than one in New Orleans. And if there was more than five, we were screwed.

I wanted to question him now. But doing so in the middle of town was not a good idea. The serum had worn off and there was no telling if the people suddenly milling around, were friend or foe.

We stopped in front of Pearl, and I urged Covington forward. "Climb up on the horse," I said, putting a little steel in my voice. I snuck a glance at Jackson. He was taking in the people surrounding us, a look of cold calculation on his face. He knew something wasn't quite right. I could also feel the walls closing in.

"Didn't you hear me!" Covington yelled, his eyes wild. "I can't leave my cousin here."

I sighed. I didn't want to have this conversation out in the open. But unless I responded, he was going to make a scene. I leaned in and whispered, "We heard you. Now please get on the horse. The sooner we are out of town, the better."

Jackson pulled a seven-inch round alloy disk out of his bag and tossed it on the ground. Gears ground as the disk expanded, enlarging to a forty-inch flat silver circle covering the ground. A metal cage shot up toward the sky, and spider legs dropped down, finally settling into a portable cage.

"Well, would you look at that," Pearl said, eyes widening.

Jackson gave her a half smile. "Courtesy of the Marshal Service."

I stared at the cage, then turned to Jackson, eyes narrowed. "So, you *do* plan on double crossing me."

"What!" Pearl rounded on him. "Why you dirty, low-down—"

Jackson raised his hand, cutting her off. "We need to get out of town. Now," he said, his jaw clenched. He walked over and none too nicely shoved Covington into the cage.

After climbing on his horse, he looked down at me. "How far?" he asked. I gave him a questioning look. "I know what you can do, Parasol. Now, how far?"

My jaw dropped. Jackson knew my secret. I wanted to stand there and try to figure out where I'd slipped. How he had figured it out. But we had gained an even larger audience. Some of the shop owners had wandered out into the open, seeming to close in on us.

"A mile," I said, and climbed on Betsy.

Jackson pulled a small, round alloy coated object out of his pocket and pressed the single green button in the center. Steam erupted from a hole on the top of the cage, and the legs moved forward, rocking back and forth. Covington held on to the bars, staring out of them like a man who had nothing left.

I had no time to change out the saddle on Betsy, so I got on my horse and followed Jackson out of town. Pearl, not caring about the noise, paced beside me.

We stopped a mile and a half out on the bayou near a burned down farmhouse. Large cypress trees obscured most of the property. But from what I could see, the place had burned down some time recently. Its charred remains still had the scorch marks of the newly burned. A half decent barn sat next to the house, so I guided Betsy and Pearl to it with Jackson following close behind me. We hadn't spoken since we left New Orleans. Which was fine with me. I was still trying to figure out how he knew about my ability to kill Soulless Ones. Sure, he hadn't come out and said it, but I knew Jackson. Knew every look, and at times, could practically read his mind.

My sister had silenced her steps when we left New Orleans. She, too, had said nothing. Covington, however, had pleaded with us to take him back. It was only after Jackson threatened him a third time that he'd quieted down.

We started for the barn, but before we got close enough, both Betsy and Ol' Nick bucked, pulling on their reins.

"Easy now," Jackson said, rubbing Nick's neck.

Betsy's gears whirred and she switched from mammal to machine. I glanced at the barn, studying the darkness inside. A breeze blew through and carried the scent of feces and blood.

I climbed down and gave her a rub before I started for the barn. Jackson and Pearl followed. When we entered, I gasped. Blood and gore covered the walls.

"Whatever happened here, happened within the past few days," I said. The woodchips and hay crunched beneath my boots as I moved farther into the space.

"You think this is the Cummings place?" Pearl asked.

"They didn't say anything about burning the house down," I said, thinking.

Jackson came to stand next to me. He surveyed the barn and then looked down at me. "You ready to talk?" he asked.

I thought about it. Was I ready to tell Jackson all my secrets? I glanced up at him, searching his eyes. If he had kept such a big secret from me, I would have been hurt. Hell, I would have been pissed. But Jackson looked at me the same way he always did, as if I meant the world to him. And if I was honest, a glimmer of those same feelings were probably reflected in my eyes as well. So, I looked away.

I glanced outside. Covington had slid down, his knees pressed into his chest, with his head resting in his hands. "Might want to let him out first."

"You trust him?" Jackson said, pulling the remote from his pocket and walking back outside.

"Yeah. He has nowhere to go."

The cage door rattled open, and Covington looked up. After a brief hesitation, he eased up and stepped out. "Why are we at the Cummings' house?" he asked.

Well, that answered one question. "Do you know what happened here?"

Covington nodded. "Mr. Cummings and his family were killed. They burned the house with them inside yesterday. Lionel said he helped." They were covering up the crime.

"Tell me about your cousin," I said, pulling my canteen out of my bag and handing it to him.

He took a long sip and handed it back. "Thank you." He pulled in a breath and let it out slowly. "I came to New Orleans because Lionel sent word that one of the relics I was searching for was in town. And I also needed a place to lie low. No one knew about Lionel, since we had been estranged for years. So, I figured it would be safe. At least until my former boss gave up looking for me."

"Did you know he put a bounty out on you?"

Covington shook his head. "I figured he'd come after me himself."

"Why?"

"Because he's a Soulless One."

"How do you know?" Jackson asked, his eyes narrowing.

Covington shivered. "Because I caught him feeding. He didn't know I was there. But . . . " He looked away. "I thought for sure he had heard me come in. The woman he was feeding from was still alive while he tore into her stomach. The sounds she made…" He closed his eyes and rubbed his arms. "I didn't think anyone could ever make those sounds. When I was finally able to move, I started to run out and saw the money on his desk. I didn't think. Just grabbed it and ran."

"Why take the money?" I asked. "And why are you buying relics from the past?"

"Because my boss was also looking for items that

belonged to Sophia MacDougall. Duncan MacDougall's great granddaughter. He was trying to find her journal."

Pearl gasped.

My grandfather had searched for the same journal when he was looking for a way to kill the Soulless Ones. He hadn't been able to find it.

Duncan MacDougall had been the first person to attempt to weigh the human soul. Some believed he was looking for a way to identify the Soulless Ones. Others believed he was a fraud and reduced his twenty-one-gram theory to mere pulp fiction. Sophia, however, knew her great grandfather's experiment was real, and it was rumored that she had found the way to identify and even kill the Soulless Ones. Some believed all her research had been lost when the world changed. But others believed the information had survived.

"Did you find it?" Pearl asked when I continued to stare at the man.

"At first all I was able to find were family heirlooms and old medical devices."

"Doesn't explain why you're looking for them," Jackson added. I had told him the story about the MacDougall bloodline a while ago.

"Because. I need to find a way to protect myself."

That would make sense. However, it didn't explain why his boss would be looking for the items too. "Did your boss ever tell you why he wanted to find Sophia's journal?"

"He said he would be able to save the world. I assumed if I could find it first, I would be able to instead."

Something about his story was off. Since his former boss was a Soulless One. One who, according to Covington, killed the innocent, his pursuits of trying to save the world didn't make sense. And why would Covington, who was trying to hide from his boss, set out to do the same? I studied him for a moment, noting the absence of sweat on him. An alarm ran through me. He caught me staring and turned away.

"How many Soulless Ones are in town?" I moved in, getting in his face. "And how do you know?" There was no way in hell he had caught a Soulless One feeding a second time. And I still didn't believe he'd caught his boss feeding either. He would have been killed.

"Three, at least." He turned, still refusing to look at me. He was lying.

I grabbed his arm and pulled him in close. "It wouldn't be a good idea to lie to me."

He swallowed, his eyes wide. He turned and took in Pearl and Jackson, who stood by, letting me do what I did best.

"Seven. At least seven."

"Why lie about the number?" Jackson bit out.

Covington tried to pull away. I held firm. "Please. My cousin has been able to keep himself under control. He shouldn't . . . " I shoved him away and walked over to my saddle bag. Pausing for a moment, I gave myself time to think. Seven meant I didn't have enough ammo to kill all of them. And if what I was thinking was true, then we were already in a great deal of danger.

"Pearl," I said.

She nodded, then got my black case out and retrieved my already loaded gun.

A cold resolve washed over me, and I pulled a vial of the red gold serum from my bag and downed the contents. Once it had worked its way through my system, Pearl handed me my gun, and I turned and looked at Covington.

A stolen soul rested inside of him.

SIX

I gave Covington a cool look and pointed my gun at him. "Care to tell me the story again?" A deadly note crept into my voice. "This time, try using the truth."

His face went through a series of emotions, each one filled with desperation, until finally, he sighed and let his mask fall. The color in his eyes bled out. His cheekbones sharpened, and his fangs snicked down. Jackson pulled his gun and pointed it at Covington. The man gave Jackson a mocking glance and shook his head. "That lead bullet won't work. Just sting a little is all."

"His gun might not work. But my sister's will. But before she kills your ass, I will make you suffer," Pearl said, moving in closer. She could make him hurt. But I needed answers first.

Covington nodded. "I believe you. But please," he raised his hands, "hear me out first."

He stared at the gun in my hand. "The sheriff smelled the silver when he showed up at Willow Sin last night. At first, he thought it was the bullets in Clarence's gun. But the officer he left outside said he could still smell silver when they took Clarence and his gun away." He stared at me, waiting for me to react. When I didn't he continued, "In exchange for my cousins life, the sheriff asked me to kill you and your companion. He was afraid you had figured out what was going on in town."

"Parasol. If you're going to kill him, I suggest you get on with it," Jackson said, his voice strained.

I kept my eyes on Covington. "Let him finish," I told Jackson.

Covington dipped his head in thanks.

"He should know silver alone won't kill the Soulless."

He glanced at Pearl. "He believes you have other means of destroying us."

I furrowed my brow. "My sister?"

He nodded. "I was supposed to plead my case. Gain your trust and sympathy. But I knew it wouldn't work."

No wonder the sheriff had been so interested in Pearl. He thought she could kill them. Not me. Her. Maybe my secret was safe.

"Did you kill the Cummings family?" I asked.

"No. The sheriff did. I tried to stop him, but the others came and restrained me. Made me watch while he slaughtered the rest of the family. Then they burned the place to the ground. My cousin and I have been in a cell ever since."

"Is the entire department Soulless Ones?" Jackson asked.

It would explain why the sheriff lied about what had killed the Cummings family.

"Yes. I believe a great many in New Orleans are. I was only able to identify the five officers in the police department. Along with the sheriff and his deputy." He hesitated, then closed his eyes and said the last in a rush. "My cousin, Lionel was changed some time ago."

"Why did you come to see the Cummings?" I asked.

"Mr. Cummings found Sophia's journal. I was supposed to meet him. I believe they got wind of what I was doing and eliminated the entire family."

Which meant the sheriff had the journal now. And if I wanted to get it, I'd have to kill him. I wished I felt good about our chances of survival. I turned to Pearl, resolve settling over me. "Send Grandpa a message. Let him know we're in New Orleans and we're surrounded."

She nodded, her face grim, and then closed her eyes. Her gears worked as she sent a message to George, my grandfather's automaton. While she did that, I turned back to the others. "Jackson. I believe you owe me a story."

"I assume you will be going next," he said, staring at Pearl.

I opened my mouth to respond, then closed it. This was going to be hard. I looked at Covington. "Are any of the girls at Willow Sin Soulless Ones?"

"No. They plan to turn the rest of the town within the week. All the ones they've managed to turn are holed up in Josephine's, waiting for the town to open again so they can feed. They want to turn Orleans into a mecca for the Soulless Ones. It gets enough tourism and wayward souls to sustain them. I saw plans to build a resort here in my boss's office."

"Then why risk coming here if you knew of your boss's plans?" I asked.

He glanced down. "I had to try and get my cousin out. He never mentioned in his telegram about the journal that he'd been turned. I assumed he was human. So, I took a chance. My plan was to get the journal and take my cousin as far away as possible. If I hadn't stopped at Willow Sin, I might have succeeded."

"Why would you stop? And why brag about your plans to Cherise?"

He gave me a pitiful smile. "Pretty girls are my weakness."

I shook my head and turned to Jackson. "How did you find out about me?"

He ran his hand down his face. "My team and I went to New Haven, Texas when we got word of a Soulless One den. One got away from us. I gave chase and stumbled onto you right after you dispatched it. I was mad at first. Hurt, even. But then…shit, Parasol. I'm tired of our on-again, off-again relationship. I want you in my life. Always have. Always will." He stared at me, letting his last words sink in.

I focused on what he first said, pointedly ignoring his last statement. We couldn't afford to get sentimental right now. If my estimates were correct, we had a horde of Soulless Ones to kill, and talking about feelings just wasn't in the cards right now. "The Marshal service is hunting the Soulless?"

He nodded. "I had wanted to recruit you. But . . . "

I shook my head and turned away. There was no way in hell I would willingly join the government.

He reached for me, and I stepped away. "We can talk about the rest later," I whispered.

"Okay. I can wait."

Pearl opened her eyes. "Grandpa says he's twelve hours out. Said for us to reserve as much of the ammo as we can and use the axe."

I nodded and turned back to Jackson. "How did you find me this time?"

"I knew you were still working for Blankeon, so I watched him, and when he hired you again, I followed. Turned out you were after the same man as me." He turned to Covington. "We knew about your boss being a Soulless One. Didn't know about you, though. We figured he had some plans, and you could give us the information we needed."

"You were stalking my sister?" Pearl asked.

Jackson shook his head. "It wasn't like that!"

After a short pause, I took them through what I knew.

"Why didn't you tell me?" Jackson asked, sounding wounded.

"I'm sorry. Our secrets were our own."

"Your secrets could have saved thousands of people,

Parasol. Can you imagine how many Soulless Ones we could have killed if we only had the knowledge?"

"They would have taken my grandpa's weapon and sold it to the highest bidder. Maybe even capturing me to ensure my grandpa's cooperation. Any weapon in the hands of the government would be deadly. Do you really believe they would have shared with the rest of the world? No, Jackson. They would have made the world pay. Their greed would have got in the way of their better judgment."

"And you think you and your grandfather can bring them down by yourselves?" he yelled.

I cringed at the anger in his tone. "Between my grand-father and I, we have killed hundreds."

"Leaving thousands more to kill," he said.

I shook my head. He was right. But I was too stubborn to admit it.

"I know we should have shared with others. But if we had, my grandpa could have been killed. I can't lose him, Jackson."

He crossed his arms.

I needed him to understand. Covington hadn't attacked us even though he was supposed to. Which meant he probably had control like my grandpa. At least I was hoping he did. "When is the last time you fed?" I asked.

"Three weeks ago. A man I caught trying to force himself on a woman. I never kill the innocent. And the pain . . . " He trailed off, looking away. "It gets better."

"Not all of the Soulless Ones are so willing to give up killing, Parasol," Jackson said.

"I know," I snapped.

He started to say something, and I lifted my hand to stop him. We were going round and round and right now, no matter what I said, Jackson wouldn't understand. "We can argue about this later. First, we need to come up with a plan."

Jackson nodded. "Do you have enough ammo?"

"No. Like Pearl said, we have to use the axe."

"Beheading?" Jackson asked.

"Yes. I have five bullets to last us until my grandfather gets here with more. If we hole up in Willow Sin, maybe we can make it through the night. Otherwise, we will have to get up real close and personal."

"I can help," Covington said.

I gave him a skeptical look. "You sure it's not another ploy to set us up?"

He turned toward the town. "Let's just say I'm motivated. I want to find a cure. And that means I have to pry that journal out of the sheriff's hands. Preferably his dead hands. He got the jump on me once, but I know he's been changed recently. I was changed over a year ago. His strength is no match for mine one-on-one."

"Why were you playing docile before?" Jackson asked.

He gave Jackson a remorseful look. "I wasn't just putting on a show for you. I needed the others to believe I was going to go along with their plan."

"Were you planning on killing us to get away?" I asked.

"No. But I did figure I could overpower you at some point." He looked at Pearl. "But when I saw your automaton—"

"Her sister," Pearl said, cutting him off.

He smiled at that. "Your sister. I knew I couldn't get away. I would have told you the truth." He looked down at the vial I'd dropped on the floor. "Does that let you see us?"

I nodded. I still wasn't ready to share everything. "Where did you send the items you purchased in the other towns?"

He rubbed the fingernail on his thumb over his eyebrow, his eyes cast to the ground. He didn't want to tell me. I could see it in his body language.

"We are going to have to start trusting one another," I said.

He bobbed his head up in down and let his hand fall to his side. "I sent them along to Ohio. My plan was to send what I got here there as well. But . . . " he trailed off.

"What's in Ohio?"

"A place I secured for me and my cousin." He shifted on his feet.

I wouldn't press. It wasn't important anyway. The only thing we had to worry about now was how to keep Ella and her girls and anyone else in town who hadn't been turned safe.

"The sheriff was right to fear you," Covington said. He stuck out his hand. "What do you say. Enemy of my enemy."

I hesitated, then extended my own. "Well. Make sure you don't double cross us."

"I won't," Covington said with conviction. "My old boss has already destroyed one town. I won't let him destroy another."

"What?" I said, gaping at him.

"This isn't the first mecca he's created."

SEVEN

Willow Sin sat in darkness. Not a good sign. Like Ella said, nothing could keep a horny man from having a good time. Either the sheriff had shut her down and decided to change the women ahead of schedule, or she'd concluded that she and her girls weren't safe, and it was better that she kept the doors locked. The latter was wishful thinking on my part. I knew that. But I also knew I was in over my head. I'd come to New Orleans to hunt one man. Now I had to try and find a way to kill—if Covington's estimates were correct—half the town.

We'd decided to enter Willow Sin from the marsh area in the back to avoid being seen. I only hoped the French doors leading into the dining room weren't too valuable, because we had no plans on knocking.

Betsy came to stand next to me. Her eyes had gone completely red. She could take care of herself. We'd left Ol' Nick at the barn. If things got bad, I'd hate to see the horse killed.

Pearl moved ahead, scouting the area. She peered down the street, scanning for people. "I count sixty people still holed up in Josephine's. The rest of the town has a few scattered folks in the shops. Six people are in Ella's," she said.

Pearl wouldn't be able to tell if the sheriff and his deputies were among that number. I added an additional six to the total. Which made absolutely no difference in the long run. Whether it was sixty or sixty-six, there was no way in hell we could manage that many.

I felt Jackson at my back. I turned and locked eyes with him. He had a look of a man not liking his odds. It seemed as if he was working through a difficult puzzle and just needed a minute to put the last few pieces together.

"Fire?" he said finally. "That's what we used in New Haven when we found a house with five of them in there."

I shook my head. "Did you confirm they were dead?"

He furrowed his brow. "How could they possibly survive?"

I sighed. "Did you see the bodies, Jackson?"

He hesitated. Then shook his head.

"They most likely walked out, found the nearest person, and fed to heal their wounds." I paused. "Although. In that weakened state, we could behead a few of them."

"We'd have to confirm everyone in there is a Soulless One," he said, giving me a questioning look.

"Right." I walked over to Betsy and pulled out my last vial of serum. "This will help you see the stolen souls inside of them."

"How will I be able to tell?" he asked, staring at the vial in my hand.

"By its constant movement and the burnt-orange color surrounding it. It will also give you extra strength in case we have to fight and help with healing." I handed it to him. "It's made of Aquagold and infused with a drop of blood and will last for eight hours."

"Whose blood?" Jackson asked, uncapping the vial.

"Do you trust me?"

He smiled. "With my life. My heart is another matter."

"This is not the time to discuss feelings," Pearl admonished. "Now drink the stuff so we can deal with these fuckers!"

Jackson nodded and downed the contents. I gave him a minute to let the stuff start working.

"Were Mr. Cummings and his family Soulless Ones?" It might have explained the burning after they were dead. Less questions that way.

Covington shook his head. "He knew that my cousin was and tried to help when he could." He turned away as if ashamed.

"How did he help?" I asked, a sick feeling filling my gut.

"He'd find the ones who couldn't be saved. The ones who were evil and—"

I held up my hand. I didn't need to know. Of course, that was the same thing my grandfather did when he needed to feed. He'd find people who he deemed evil and take their souls. I never asked him how he found them. I didn't want to know. Didn't want to dwell on the fact that my grandfather was out there passing judgment on others.

Hoping that his conclusions about the people he killed was correct. Even one innocent soul was too much.

"We'll need kerosene," I said, refocusing on the plan. "But first, I want to make sure Ella and her girls are okay."

"Now or never," Jackson said, his voice a little hoarse. "This shit you gave me is worse than moonshine."

"You get used to it," I said, and started forward. Jackson held the axe, and I had my gun out. Pearl would break down the door just in case Ella had her shotgun. While Covington would have survived the bullet wound, I didn't want him down for even a second. He needed to back us up when shit hit the fan.

We arrived at the French doors. Pearl peered inside and, once satisfied the room was clear, she placed both hands on the doors and shoved. The doors splintered, the sound echoing as glass and wood split apart as if blown up with dynamite.

Someone screamed, and I rushed in, my boots crunching on the debris. I emerged in the front hall and found one of the officers with his hand around Cherise's neck. Two other officers were behind him, pushing their way inside. When he saw me, he tossed her to the side like she was a rag doll. She crashed onto the couch her body going limp.

He rushed me, knocking me to the ground before I could squeeze off a single shot. His dead, soulless eyes stared down at me, his razor-sharp teeth gnashing as he tried to get to my neck. Rancid breath washed over me, making my stomach turn. I shoved with all my strength, gaining some purchase. But not enough. I heard a commotion behind me and had only a brief second to fear for Jackson.

My gun had been knocked from my hand. But I did have my blade. Keeping one arm across his throat, I snatched the elk-handled knife from its sheath and buried it in the back of his neck.

An unholy howl erupted from his mouth—sounding like the dead crying into the wind.

Blood ran down, spilling onto my face and getting in my eyes, leaving me temporarily blinded.

I yanked the knife out again, ready to plunge it back into him, but suddenly his weight was gone. I swiped the blood from my face and looked up. My sister held him in her hands.

"Get off my sister, you evil fuck!" she yelled, then ripped his head from his shoulders.

I thought he'd been on me for minutes; turned out it'd been mere seconds. The other two deputies were squared off with Jackson and Covington. And Ella stood at the foot of the stairs, shotgun in hand, pointed at the deputies. Her hands might have been trembling, but her eyes were dead calm.

I jumped up and retrieved my gun. After checking on Cherise, I pointed my gun at the deputies too.

"Save your bullets, darlin'," Jackson said with steel in his voice.

I glanced at the deputies. Even though they clearly had

the upper hand, they didn't move forward. Why weren't they attacking?

"Waiting for someone?" I asked.

One of the deputies turned his soulless eyes to me and smiled, his killing teeth on morbid display. "Your soul will be so sweet."

"No. Not really," I said, and I put a bullet in his head. He must have believed I had only silver because he didn't even attempt to move. I stepped back, covered my ears, and waited.

When a Soulless One dies, it sounds like fallen angels crying to heaven to let them in again. The first time I'd heard the sound, I'd wept, believing my life was going to end. My grandfather, once he had been turned, explained it to me. The Soulless were always seeking that part of them that had been taken. Always looking for the one thing humanity needed the most. Their soul. And for some…their salvation. Once the soul is gone, the pain is too much to bear. But when they feel the cold hand of death, that pain magnifies. Without a soul, one cannot reflect on a life well lived. Or hope for something more to come. The Soulless know the only thing waiting for them is pain.

The deputy opened his mouth and sang. The sound was like claws running down my back. An old primal fear surfaced, screaming for me to run and seek safety and hide. The cries sounded as if all the souls he had consumed rang out, filling the small space. From the bullet wound in his head, his flesh began to eat away at itself, caving into his body as if something were eating him alive. Blood ran down the wound. Its slow trickle reminded me of a snake slowly slithering down his now blackened face. Like lava crawling along volcanic rock.

His partner turned rabid eyes toward me, teeth gnashing, looking for blood. He started to charge, but before he could take a single step, Jackson, in one mighty swing, chopped the man's head off.

Giving him no chance to sing the song of the dead and dying. Like the deputy whose head my sister took off. It was a mercy, really. One I didn't want to extend, but we had to in order to survive the night.

"What was that sound?" Jackson asked, rubbing his ears.

"Their death song. The serum I gave you allows you to hear it."

He nodded and turned away.

Ella gasped, her shotgun clattering to the floor. She sank down on the steps while her gaze darted around the room. When it landed on Cherise, she surged up and ran to the woman. "Is she dead?" she asked, sobbing. She seemed afraid to check. All the grit and determination I'd seen in her earlier had completely drained from the woman. I didn't blame her. Seeing the Soulless die would do that to a person.

I joined her next to Cherise and pressed two fingers to the unconscious woman's neck. Her pulse was a bit thready, but at least she was still among the living and had her soul.

I placed my hand on Ella, trying to reassure her. "She'll be fine. At least . . . I hope so."

She nodded. A single tear slid down her face. "I promised I would protect them."

"And you will," I said. "Why were the deputies here?"

"Sheriff Longfellow called earlier, said the deputies would be stopping by to keep an eye on things." Her mouth thinned, and anger sparked in her eyes. "I didn't think nothing of it. Thought the bastard was just trying to destroy my business like the others in town. I sent Cherise down." She placed her hand over Cherise's. "Figured she could let them in." She looked up suddenly. "Someone destroyed my back door."

"That was me," Pearl said as she moved the last deputy outside and shut the door.

There was no easy way to tell her what was going on. Honestly, I was somewhat surprised she hadn't figured it out already. But I told her. And when I was finished, a cold resolve filled her eyes. She stood up and looked at Jackson. "Can you move her upstairs?" she asked, dipping her head toward Cherise. "I need to get the other girls prepared. What weapons do we have?"

I showed them my dual-barreled gun I used to kill the Soulless. "This gun has been modified to hold and fire two different types of ammunition. Silver and a specially made bullet that contains Aquagold and the soul of a dying Soulless One. Once combined, the two work together to kill the Soulless by eroding the stolen soul inside of them.

I also have my Sig pistol that will give them a bit of a

sting. Unless you have silver bullets on hand that can fit." I thought about the Aquagold she had in her coffee machine. While it would work better to have a capsule made of the stuff with a tainted soul inside, it couldn't hurt to have the bullets coated in the water. Afterall, the strange substance did seem to work for everything.

"I have silver bullets," she said, offering no explanation. Another surprise given our earlier conversation about the Soulless Ones. It also made me wonder why the sheriff never got wind of her bullets before. Especially if he smelled mine when he showed up after Clarence's death.

"Soak them in the water before you load them in the gun." I lifted my chin toward Covington. "Try not to shoot him. He's on our side." At least I hoped he was.

She gave him a hard look and nodded. Jackson returned with the rest of the girls in tow. Linda, one of the girls I'd met earlier, showed Ella a gun. "I have this," she said hesitantly.

"What kind of ammo do you have?" I asked.

She looked away. "Silver bullets. Since the Soulless took my husband, I've always carried silver."

Ella gave her a look filled with concern and understanding. "Get the Aquagold. We have bullets to purify."

I smiled. Ella, it would seem, missed her life in the church. Made me wonder what happened that drove her away from her religion. Linda rushed to the back room. We moved about, cataloging our weapons, getting ourselves ready for a long night. Ella, thankfully, had some kerosene, and once we were armed, we would head over to Josephine's to set the place on fire. That was the plan, at least.

"Parasol," Pearl screamed, stopping me in my tracks. "They're coming!"

The deputy's death song had brought the others.

We were out of time.

Pearl moved away from the window and stood by the door. I whistled, and Betsy clopped into the room through the broken French doors. "When they come in, let Betsy do most of the work. Neck and head shots will slow them down. If you can remove the head, good. If not, step away. They recover quickly. If you feel as if you're getting boxed in, get behind my sister or my horse. They can't be killed."

Jackson hefted his axe, handing his gun off to one of the girls.

Linda had brought the Aquagold out and dumped all the bullets in it. Pearl positioned herself in front of the door. Betsy blocked the back.

I glanced out the window at the Soulless Ones standing in the middle of the street, their dead eyes transfixed on Willow Sin. "They're not moving," I said. "We have time to secure the back." Parasol shoved the furniture toward the side door leading to the dining room and kitchen. After piling it up, she went upstairs and retrieved Cherise. The girl, while dazed, had come around.

Jackson came and stood next to me. "What are they waiting for?"

No sooner had he asked, Sheriff Longfellow's voice rang out. "Frank Covington. We had ourselves a deal. Seems you have broken it."

I turned and looked at Covington.

"But I'm a fair man. What say you rid us of our visitors, and in return, I will give you your cousin. Unharmed."

"Enemy of my enemy," I said, reminding him of our bargain.

He dipped his head once in acknowledgement, then moved toward the window and peered out. "They have him on his knees out front. They also have a gun trained on his head." He turned and regarded me. "How did you learn how to kill us with silver?"

I had no choice but to tell him the truth.

He gave me a look of confusion. "But that's how I was turned. He bit into my neck, spilling my blood. When my soul had detached from me, he took it and shoved a another one in me. I could feel the soul twisting inside of me. Changing my body." He looked off. "The pain was intense. It was like my body wanted to reject it. Soon, the ache dulled, and I could bare it. But only for a short while. I had to consume another soul."

I nodded, let out a sigh, and continued. "My grandfather learned that what makes you can also kill you, given the right circumstances. It's the water and the silver combined with the rotten soul. He believes the Aquagold is a sort of purification, and it prevents the stolen souls from staying bound to you. So the pain quite literally eats you alive."

It was his turn to nod. He closed his eyes. "When we're shot with silver, I can feel the stolen soul pulling away from me, allowing for the pain. But it doesn't last long. And eventually, I'm able to re-fuse it back to myself." He opened his eyes. "Even my old employer didn't know, aside from beheading, how to kill us." He paused, his eyes filling with understanding. "Of course, Bobby Daring, the famed inventor would devise a way to destroy us."

"He's one of you," I said, adding a note of pleading to my voice. "We are also searching for the cure."

A howl ripped through the air, and we rushed to the window. The sheriff, probably tired of waiting, had shot his cousin. "Forgive my cruelty," I said, turning back to Covington. "But it's time to give the sheriff your answer."

"He shot Lionel." The color in his eyes bled away, his fangs dropped down, and his fingers lengthened. "The sheriff is mine."

I squeezed his shoulders, reassuring him, and turned to my sister. "Pearl. Can you take Betsy and go get his cousin?"

She smiled. "Looks like I get to go introduce myself to a few of the good folks here in New Orleans." She patted Betsy. "Come on, Betsy. Let's go move the crowd."

Betsy neighed, rising up. Her eyes blazed red.

I wished my sister and Betsy's efforts would take all of them down, but likely only a few would suffer under their ministrations. We had to change our plans. I looked at Ella. She held her shotgun half-raised, waiting for the battle to begin. A look of pure grit and determination had taken over the fear in her eyes. But I also saw a flicker of resolve. As if she, too, had calculated our odds and came up with craps. I wanted to give her hope. But all I could muster was a slim chance. A possibility that heavily relied upon many of the Soulless not wanting to die.

Which meant I had to prove we had the means to kill them.

Plan solidified, I walked over to her. "Ella, I know you worked hard for this place. But sadly, the only way I see out of this situation is if we can lure enough of them inside and burn the place down. I need to separate the fearless from those who wish to live."

Tears laced with pain and frustration filled her eyes. She glanced around the room as if she would never see it again, cataloging each joy, each emotion, each loss. Finally, her gaze settled on the girls in the room, all of whom had taken up some weapon of sort, ready to follow her into battle.

She nodded once to them and then turned back to me. "If we live, I can rebuild. Make it better than it was."

I squeezed her shoulder, letting her see the vow in my eyes that I would do everything in my power to keep her alive. "Thank you." I turned away. "Pearl, I'm going out with you."

"Now hold on," Jackson said, moving toward me. "Like you said, your sister and Betsy can't be killed. But you, darlin', can." I saw the fear of my death in his eyes, along with other things I wasn't ready to acknowledge.

"No, Jackson. I have no plans to get myself killed. In order for me to weed a few of them out, I need to give them a demonstration." I lifted my gun. "They believe only Pearl can kill them. I need to prove them wrong. Like they used to say, 'I can show ya better than I can tell ya.'"

Jackson reluctantly nodded. And then he gave me one of his smiles. The one he reserved when he was about to get into some devilish deeds. "Good plan, darlin'. Mind if I come outside and watch your back?"

"There you go thinking my sister weak-willed again," Pearl said, a smile on her face.

"Not weak," Jackson said, still staring at me. "Just want to make sure I'm there when she needs me." He wasn't talking about the fight we were heading into, and we both knew it.

I placed a hand on his arm. "Well, Jackson, I believe I can handle myself. But," I leaned in, my lips a bare whisper from his, "I will let you know when I need you." I moved back and smiled. "Take care of things here. Help them spread the kerosene. Once I kill one of them, things are going to move quick. I need everyone to be ready."

He winked at me. "Will do, darlin'." Before I could turn away, Jackson pulled me to him and took my mouth, hard. The kiss lasted only a second, but its effects would carry me for the rest of the night. One of the girls whistled, and I turned away, not wanting him to see the longing in my eyes.

Steeling my spine, I stepped toward the front door. It had gone quiet outside. They were waiting. Probably giving us time to work through the inevitability of our deaths. A cold smile spread across my face. If I hadn't promised Covington I'd let him kill the sheriff, I would have put a bullet in his head first. Instead, it looked like I was going to have to settle for his deputy.

I looked at Pearl. "Ready?"

She smiled at me. "Sister, I was made to be ready."

I kicked open the door and stepped out into the street. My eyes skipped over the other Soulless and found the deputy standing close to the sheriff with a smug look on his face.

I aimed my gun.

He smirked.

I put a bullet in his head.

And laughed as he started his death song.

They stood stunned as the deputy fell to his knees and his body began rotting. Even the sheriff watched in fear as one of his own sang its last note of life. But that shock didn't last long. And when it ended, Betsy charged out, more machine than animal, and plowed through the waiting crowd.

Pearl, filled with a wicked happiness, walked up to the first Soulless One and extended her arm. "Name's Pearl," she said and ripped the man's arm clean off. He screamed, not a death song but one filled with pain, and lunged for her. She removed his head with ease and continued forward, introducing herself to as many as she could. Paving a way for me to get to Lionel.

I would have left the sheriff alone. I had no plans to even engage the man. But as I ran toward Covington's now recovered cousin, he stepped in my path.

"Should have killed you on sight," he said, his voice filled with rage.

I lifted my gun and aimed. "That was your mistake."

He rushed me. It took me by surprise. I landed on the

ground, hitting my head hard. Chaos ensued around me. Yet, I couldn't move. A ringing started in my ears, and the next thing I knew, the sheriff had sunk his teeth into my neck. Pain exploded down my back, and the sickly-sweet smell of copper filled the space around me. I'd lost my gun again and had no way of reaching the knife around my thigh.

It took me a minute to realize the sheriff hadn't done any more than bite me. He held me there like I was a damn chew toy, while Pearl and Betsy continued to plow through the crowd. Out of the corner of my eye, I watched as Lionel stumbled into view. He held a large rock in his hand. The pressure on my neck eased, and the sheriff unclamped his jaw, turning. He must have sensed Lionel. But before he could turn fully, Lionel brought the rock down on his head.

Over and over again, he beat the man's head in. Blood and brain matter rained down on me while I lay pinned underneath the sheriff's now dead weight. When he opened his mouth, I knew I was in trouble. The first notes of his death song punched into my ears and destroyed my hearing. Someone yanked me up, and I ripped the knife from my sheath and turned to my would-be attacker. Jackson raised his hands to stop me from stabbing him.

His mouth moved, but I couldn't hear what he was saying. Finally, he jerked his head over his shoulder, and I took in Willow Sin now engulfed in flames.

I scanned the street, looking for Ella and her girls, and found them standing behind Betsy, weapons raised. Ella stood in the middle of the milieu, her shotgun smoking as she aimed and shot like a woman who had stepped straight out of the Wild West.

I needed to help. But I'd lost my sense of hearing.

Bodies lay strewn across the street. But still more than twenty Soulless Ones were up and fighting. I had no idea how many had entered Willow Sin, but it had to have been enough for them to set the place on fire.

My gun lay a few feet away. After picking it up, I secured it and worked quickly through another plan. "Watch my back," I yelled and dove into the fight.

The Soulless Ones, both man and woman, saw me coming and paused. My demonstration had obviously done a good job of instilling some fear of me in them. Good. I could use that. Pearl stepped over, covered in blood, holding a man's limb by the hand. She looked crazed.

"They're fallin', Parasol. But not staying down. Can't kill them all," she said, her voice muted. Sounds slowly crept back, and I surveyed the bodies on the ground. She was right; they were mending themselves back together.

"Start taking heads," I said. I rushed to the first one trying to stand and buried my blade in the middle of its neck, wrenching it out through the side. When she started to sing her death song, Jackson severed what remained, and we moved to the next one.

Too much blood and too many bodies, but we worked through them slowly, with Pearl helping and Ella still firing her shotgun. One of her girls stood next to her with shells in her hand, giving them to Ella when she ran out. Trusting they had things in hand, I kept working my way through the bodies.

Halfway up the street, I spotted Covington and his cousin. They were surrounded by a large group. One look told me they hadn't been with the original ones who had surrounded Willow Sin.

"You're a traitor, Lionel. You know what's at stake," the one in the lead said. "We would have had access to more souls than we could possibly consume."

"To what end?" Lionel asked, clearly exasperated.

"End?" He looked at Covington. "Did you know the bitch could kill us? Is that what you two are after? Death?"

"If they are, I am more than willing to give it to them."

I stepped out of the shadows and moved into the weak light. Each of them turned in unison, taking me in. Jackson hefted his axe over his shoulder, and I lifted my gun, aiming at the leader. "Shame I wasn't invited to this party," I said, sinking menace into my voice.

The leader sniffed the air, his dead eyes locked with mine. "I smell silver. But what else is in that gun? And why do you smell like us?"

I didn't answer. Only waited. There were eight of them and four of us. Yet I got the feeling these ones were much older than the others, who had rushed toward their demise. The ones in front of us had more calculation in their eyes.

"How old are you?" I asked.

He smiled, showing off his razor-sharp teeth. "Old enough to have seen the Middle Ages."

"So. You don't need to kill?"

He laughed. The sound raked across my skin, digging into my soul. "No. I can go months without feeding." He leaned forward as if he would pounce. I leveled the gun, readying the bullet. "But why should I?"

That was his warning. And because I was expecting it, I managed to squeeze off a shot. Sadly, it went wide, missing him as he took me down. The woman had moved, pouncing on Jackson. She raised her claws, ready to rip into him, and he brought the axe handle up just in time to stop the first blow. While the serum had given us added strength, it wouldn't be enough.

The man had managed to scrape his claws against my side. I surged up, bucking under his weight as his hand came down for a second time, trying to sink into my side. Frank wrapped his arm around the man's neck in an attempt to remove him from me. But the Soulless One was much too powerful. He turned and raked his claws across Covington's stomach, spilling his guts.

Covington stumbled back, trying to hold his insides in. Before the man could resume his attack on me, I managed to shove him, my back scrapping against the stones as I slid a few inches away. I had my gun ready, and when he lunged, I fired. The bullet sank in, and I jumped up and covered my ears.

The woman who had been attacking Jackson screamed and started for me.

A hole appeared in her head, and she dropped to the ground and started her song.

It took me a minute to realize I hadn't fired. Only a few seconds more to spot my grandfather riding in on his white horse.

Pearls heavy footfalls clanged against the cobblestone as she rounded the corner. "Well, looks like Granddad has arrived," Pearl said, coming to stand by me. She had a different bloody arm in her hand. I never understood her fascination with limbs. But right now, I wasn't going to question it. I was too busy staring at my grandfather as he fired three more shots, taking down three additional Soulless Ones.

The last few started to run, but a man with long red hair stepped out of the shadows and sliced off the head of the first one to cross his path. He didn't stop. His dance was fluid as he moved from one to the next until all their heads rested on the ground.

When he was done, he straightened and dipped his head toward my grandfather, who had climbed down off his horse and was now staring at me with his familiar brown eyes.

"Granddaughter," he said. "I received your message." He stared at the wound on my side, his lips thinned in anger.

A single tear slipped from my eyes. I gripped my injured side and stumbled toward him.

"Have you drunk the serum?" he asked, his familiar clover scent washed over me.

I nodded while I stared up at him. The wound on my neck was already healing over. Sadly, while my grandfather's blood would heal me, the injuries I received would still leave a scar.

He removed my arm and studied the claw marks on my stomach. "I'll have to reinforce the leather on your clothing. My new friend has devised a way to make his battle clothes stronger. Able to repel most anything."

"That will help." I sighed, biting back the pain. "Pearl said it would take you longer to arrive."

He stepped back and looked at me. "I got word of what was going on here. Modified Gertrude some so that she could get us here faster. Of course, George didn't need much changing."

As soon as my grandfather said his name, George came stomping into view. "Well, this all looks much tamer than Pearl said it would be." He looked over at Pearl. "You indicated there were well over sixty. I count eight."

"Just like you to show up after we killed all of them," Pearl said, waving the limb she was carrying.

"I believe Johnny Day killed three and Mr. Daring killed four. That leaves one between you and Parasol." He looked over and spotted Jackson. "Oh my, I see that one has returned."

I smiled and turned to my grandfather. "This is Jackson, Grandpa." I signaled for Jackson to join us. "Jackson, this is my grandfather, Bobby Daring."

Jackson nodded and dipped his head toward the red-haired man. "I assume that's Johnny Day."

The man saluted us with his sword and walked away.

"Yes," my grandfather said. "I found him a few months ago chopping off the heads of the Soulless. Thought it best to employ him."

"Does he know what you are?" I asked, eyeing the man, who had sheathed his sword.

"He does." My grandfather didn't offer any further information. That was okay. I would find out about this Johnny Day soon enough.

"The rest of the bodies are back there, George," Pearl said.

"Are they dead?" he asked.

"No. But they sure are hurting."

He looked down at the arm she held in her hand. "And missing quite a few limbs, I suppose."

Pearl smiled. "Figured I'd introduce myself."

"Mr. Daring, sir. Do you wish to take their souls?" George asked.

My grandpa nodded, his eyes on Covington, who was just now coming around.

"He's a friend," I said, stepping into his line of sight. I looked around and found his brother slowly easing up. They must have gotten him down as well. "So is the other one. His cousin."

"Very well," my grandfather said.

I led them to the remaining Soulless Ones. Ella and her girls stood in the middle of the street, eyes darting from one body to the next. I was proud and amazed that they had managed to hold their own. Betsy stood nearby, her red gaze taking in the entire scene. When she saw me, she trotted over, shifting back to her more friendly horse form.

"I'll have to get you an apple soon," I said, rubbing her bloody neck. She had done some damage and would need a bath. Some of the Soulless Ones were having a hard time pulling themselves together thanks to her hooves. Others wouldn't be getting up again.

I went over to Ella and her girls. They stared at me out of eyes full of delirium and madness. They had survived a battle; now they would have to endure the emotional fallout.

"You okay?" I asked, staring at the building. The flames had died down. The smoke covered the area in ash.

Ella rested the butt of her shotgun on the ground and belted out a humorless laugh. "Yeah. Let me get back to you on that." She glanced at her girls. "They're safe. We're safe. That's all that matters."

I signaled to the still burning building. "What will you do?"

She shrugged. "Rebuild."

"Here?" I asked.

She gave me a half smile. "Best place in town."

I nodded, thinking about Covington's employer. He would want to know what had happened to his Mecca. Might even send some of his henchman down to find out. I wished I had asked more questions of the older Soulless Ones. Wished I could have figured out how they fit into all of this. Covington said this wasn't the only Mecca his old boss had created for the Soulless. Which meant I'd have to destroy the other ones as soon as I could.

I turned and watched as my grandfather raked his claws over the necks of the Soulless that hadn't been killed. When their death song rang out, he opened a cylindrical tube, and a burnt-orange mist was sucked up inside.

When he was finished, Pearl and George piled the bodies in the middle of the street and lit them on fire. We all stood around, watching the flames dance across the cobblestone, thankful we had survived.

My grandfather came to stand next to me. "What now, Granddaughter?"

I looked across the flames and found Jackson watching me. "Now, I find a way to destroy the other Meccas that have been created."

He nodded, following my gaze. "Will your friend help?"

I smiled. "He told me he'll protect me always. So, I guess that's a yes."

"Smart man."

I turned to him, studying his face. "What will you do now?"

He glanced around, taking in the mishmash of buildings lining Bourbon Street. "I need to settle somewhere. Continue studying the Aquagold and helping you in your search. You wouldn't believe the Soulless I have encountered. Ones just like me who want to merely exist in this world. And if I could find a cure, or even a way to sustain the souls we take, maybe we can coexist one day."

I pointed toward Covington. "I believe he and his cousin could help."

I told him about their findings and Sophia MacDougall's journal.

"I look forward to seeing it," he said, a smile playing across his face. "Will you stay long?"

"No. Just long enough to set things right."

I would stay long enough to help Ella and my grandfather rebuild New Orleans. Then, once the other meccas were destroyed, I would resume my hunt for the very first Soulless One. The one who had started it all when he sold his soul.

Cain.

My name is Carla Vonzale Lewis and I like my martinis shaken . . . never stirred.

Carla was born in Georgia, but please don't mistake her for a Georgia peach. She's more like a prickly pear. Speaking of being born, someone asked her recently if she remembered her birth. And she had to say, "Yes, I do remember that handsy doctor pulling me out into the cold. Right Bastard!!!"

Despite being born in the South, she grew up in California. Every once in a great while she gets to experience all four seasons. But mostly, it's just heat.

When not writing, Carla enjoys reading, binge watching shows on Netflix, and trying to convince her husband that getting a dog is a wonderful idea.

And one day, she will discover how many licks it actually takes to get to the center of a Tootsie Pop.

CONNECT WITH C. VONZALE

cvonzalelewis.com

facebook.com/CVLauthor

instagram.com/carlavlewis

pinterest.com/carlamc30/boards

bookbub.com/profile/c-vonzale-lewis

MORE FROM C. VONZALE LEWIS

Blood and Sacrifice Chronicles

Lineage

Zealot

Tribe (2022)

Anthologies

Masks

Love on Main

Flicker

Link by Link

The Rogue of Vangard
by Nicholas J. Evans

ONE

The battered bronze carapace of the rotary-cycle rattled dangerously under my feet.

Every bolt and screw shifted in loud clinks and clanks to let me know, in their own metallic language, that I would soon be an unrecognizable pile of goo on the distant street below.

"Come on, you *pile of parts*," I shouted to no one at all, foregoing much more colorful terms. "Come on, Come on!"

My fingers tightened around the lift console. The vibration of the steam engine reverberated up the steering shaft and through my gloves, traveling upward further until my teeth clicked against each other rhythmically. I dared not look below, but I was not much for *dares* and decided to do it anyway only to find the ground racing toward me by the second. The rooftops were closing in around me like a prison, and I pulled the console in desperation for it to just push up a little higher. My heart beat thumped rougher and quicker until it was echoing into the chasm of my throat. I swallowed hard, inhaled even harder, and concentrated on the situation at hand.

Behind me, a posse consisting of a half dozen black rotary-cycles were closing in fast. Their riders hurled balls of rotating flame at me that whizzed by with enough ambient heat to nearly singe my facial hair. I quickly turned around and reached out toward them with an open palm, the brown glove on my hand made a *hiss* sound as several metallic coils and tubes released steam on the backside just below my knuckles. There, an orb sat in a translucent blue that faintly glowed in a glacial coolness, and each of the coils fed on that soft light in turn.

In my palm, a cone-shaped blast of spiraling ice forcefully spat outward and overtook three of the six assailants. The veins of frost spread rapidly over the front propellers and wings of their newer-model rotary-cycles before encroaching on the riders themselves.

They dropped to the ground in a three-pack of cold ones. Once hasty, humming machines now turned to silent blocks of ice that noiselessly plummeted until a loud *thud* echoed skyward. Violence was never my *forte*, yet if the moment called for it then I would answer tenfold. Still, I could not watch their meteoric fall to the cobbled streets, and I quickly turned back to the view in front of me. Their shouts a moment later told me that they had survived, luckily, and I left them in the wake of steam that puffed from the rotary-cycle exhaust.

"We need backup!" I heard one of my tag-alongs call out. "He's got a Shiver Attunement!"

"Spread out around him!" Yet another joined in, this one had more of a bellowing tone like that of an opera vocalist. "Flank him from the sides! His *junker* of a cycle is going to drop at any time now!"

Funny, I thought as I pressed my boot down harder on the steam pedal to trigger just a bit more speed. *I thought I was dropping right now, actually.*

We hovered over Main Street, and I just barely missed glancing blows from tall, flickering gas light poles as I descended further. I spared a quick glance back again only to find them descending with me, their black suits nearly swallowed by the backdrop of a midnight sky behind our convoy. More twirling balls of flame came close to scorching my machine, until one of the suits sent a fastball in the style of America's favorite past time that smacked into the tail-end of the rotary-cycle; a debris spray of flame exploded, and a few small flares singe the tail of my overcoat.

I turned to watch the deep brown of the coat turn an ashy black as I smacked out the flames. While turned, I rattled off another fountain of ice. While not as effective as the *baseball boy* behind me, it struck well enough to completely freeze over his propeller and send him tumbling across the wet pavement below.

When I spun back around, I had barely enough time to ponder my next move as a wall of tall buildings blocked off the end of the road. That sight put a boulder in my throat and set my heart fluttering on a panicked autopilot. With hands firmly pulling the steering console again, I snatched a few precious moments to bowl around my ideas before myself, *and* the two remaining suits, became heaps of sprockets and gears against someone's front door.

Option one was my favorite. Not practical, but I always loved a bit of romanticized late-night combat on a rain covered street. This is where I bailed, gracefully, from my cycle and face them both head on. My Attunements against theirs.

But option two allowed for some sense of anonymity that would go great with my future. And, with a sigh, I chose option two.

A push of my left boot on another pedal, and the brakes slammed the engine to a halt.

I jerked forward with the sudden stop of motion and bashed my chest on the steering console, knocking the wind from my lungs in an invisible plume. A small price to pay, as the other two bellowed briefly before smashing into the wall of buildings before us. The thunderous boom of their cycles blowing apart into fragments was enough to wake the dead, but I was happy to see them both bail in enough time to not completely die like smashed insects. Instead, they smacked to the ground in scrapes and tumbles that most likely destroyed their suits along with their bones.

They'll live, I told myself as a self-satisfactory grin pushed itself out from under my mustache. As stated, I was not one for violence but that did not mean the *thrill* of victory was lost on me entirely.

My cycle dropped to the ground in a thud, and I heard the insides shift and snap on the impact. Each sound of its destruction hurt deep in my soul. I had that particular cycle for a couple of years now, and I tended to go through them pretty fast, so we built up a man-machine connection. I myself was unharmed. My boots activated the two Gust Attunements hidden inside the heels that caused me to hover in mid-air as my transport dropped. Instead, I was carried gracefully downward on invisible jets of warm, rushing air.

When my feet touched down on the slick pavement, it was just in time for me to hear the painful groans of my two assailants. That was my que to hit the highest of crescendos and exit stage left before a worried citizen decided to be overly helpful. Luckily, the dark alleys and humming steam pipes made for the perfect cover.

I ducked off into a nearby darkened alleyway and let the moist, humid air of the city fill my lungs. I exhaled with pure relief. My gloved hand, encrusted with the feedback of a nearly depleted Shiver Attunement orb, crept under my jacket lapel and retrieved another glossy orb. Translucent rainbows swirled inside of it as a warm, white glow radiated from its core. It jolted a smile from just below my facial fur, and I tucked it away as I strolled down the alley. Locusts of bright joy fluttered around my stomach when I thought of just how close I was to losing this precious artifact.

Yet, I *won*.

Twilight seemed to dome off the city as steam stacks rose to meet the stars.

I was far below them, gazing up at a brilliant sky from the ambient glow of a steam light post. The city is quiet, all but the whir and stir of copper pipes that spread out from every home and building like spiderwebs as they root their way down into cobblestone roadway. The alley I emerged from sat blackened and hollow beside me as I removed a long, narrow cigarette from my jacket and placed it between my pursed lips like a gentle, deadly kiss. From that darkness just beyond my vision, sirens bloomed, and footsteps pounded against the streets giving me the notion that it would only be a matter of time until they got a little *too* curious about this alleyway.

That is fine, I told myself.

From another pocket I removed the flicker-clicker; a small oval object of brass with steam tubes no larger than a hornet antenna. These tubes weaved into the marble-sized Scorch Attunement orb and crept like ivy up to the surface, producing a small but controlled flame. I pushed the wrapped tobacco to the flame and let the smoke perform a luxurious ballet over my taste buds. It pirouetted down into my lungs, where it had a brief intermission before performing the routine in reverse. The gray plume fell from my lips and climbed into the twinkling sky as the sirens scream louder in the distance.

A two-seater locomoti-cart pulled up with a grind and hiss, and a burly man poked his head out of the driver's side window. His steam stack gives two identical piercing shouts in succession which he accented with a half-cocked grin.

"Hey, pal, need a lift?" he asked in a voice that resembled stones scratching together, and the whistle of the steam engine capped off his sentence.

I shrugged and took a minute to size the man up, looking him over for signs of imminent danger. *That's just how I am, cautious and collected.* If I had not been, I would not have made it as far as I have. The translucent rainbow orb in my jacket would prove that.

The driver had a bushy beard of blossoming brown coils that wrapped the bottom half of his melon-shaped head. A small set of bronze-rimmed glasses, with several interchangeable magnifying lenses, sat on a bulbous red nose and rested under bushy brows. His smile was kind, but the chest hair finding new life sprouting from his tunic told me he didn't care all too much about appearances. While a grin and rosy cheeks may seem a warm welcome, a smile is an accessory worn just as a necklace would be to some people. People like *me,* for instance.

I smiled in return.

My bowler cap was removed from my head as I took a bow, swiftly catching it with a graceful hand out of overbearing showmanship. The driver chuckled, and he acknowledged with a tip of his tall, burgundy top hat that was embellished with decorative copper gears.

"I'd appreciate that, sir," I said with a chime to my voice. "What's the charge?"

He laughed; a bellowing tummy laugh that reddens his already pre-reddened cheeks.

"Aye, no charge this time around. Hear the sneaky *bobs* from a mile around. Wouldn't want to leave ya at their mercy, I wouldn't." He gestured for me to come around and climb in the locomoti-cart passenger side. "Besides, if ya don't mind me pickin' up my next fare down the way a bit, it gives me some company."

I smirked, a little more genuine this time, and passed him a nod before wrapping around the pointed front as the train whistle howled again. I pulled open the door and climbed aboard as the wheels crackled over the cobblestones.

The locomoti-cart was a work of wondrous fascination at one time. An early solution to the ever-growing power of the steam engine against the rapidly aging horse carriage. A train with just slightly more maneuverability and a smaller design, which made local transportation a thriving business rivaling even that of the long-distance locomotive. This particular one was an older model, with rust chewing at the spokes and the wood cart stained from years of routine weathering. Still, I could appreciate the business acumen of this driver even with the older cart, as it was one more vehicle than I had now.

"Normally, I sit in the cart for these things. It's a nice change sitting up front," I tossed over to him in polite conversation.

"I leave the cart for the drunks on my pub passes, if ya still got yer lights about ya then the front of the train it is!"

After a nod of acknowledgment, I enjoyed the silence for a couple of minutes as we strolled along down the street, letting the sirens grow distant and fade the further we moved from my wreckage. I haven't come to this city in years, *years and years* to be exact, and my last trip ended something like this one had begun oddly enough. Still, I had what I came for now, and it was as good of a time as any to take another hiatus from the bustle of Vangard.

This city had become something else entirely since last time. A creature of evolution, growing and expanding until there was little that remained to satiate its thirst or hunger. More shops, more trinkets, more *steam*. Most businesses were closed this late under the moon, except for a few pubs and local eateries, but I could see what they all sold. Cheaply made rotary-cycles that looked like they were ready to fall apart before leaving the ground, a shop dedicated to selling augmented rifle and sword combinations known simply as Barrel-Blades, and a few clothing stores that I could hardly tell apart.

Sometimes we passed people wandering the cobbled roads of Vangard as if the midnight and midday were twin siblings. Long coats of brown, red or black trimmed with copper and brass, ruffled tunics below them that met with pants that apparently held the primary purpose of carrying a few too many belts and satchels until the pants ended in large, outlandish boots. All of it accented with far too many golden colored ornaments, and that goes without mentioning the *monocles on monocles on monocles* that reflected the steam lamp light. Many cities and towns here carried these fashions, and it spread from commoner to nobility like a starving plague. While it was not lost on me entirely, my own fashion choices blending nicely with their own, it still was a sight to behold for any outsider.

And all of that is without mentioning the corsets, the dresses, the hats, the curled facial hair and dyed locks, and, of course, the Attunement orbs. The hues and auras of Attunement orbs crossed over a wide variety of the color spectrum. They would span from dangerously deadly, as my own and my *followers* from earlier, to the mundane such as the Gust Attunement orbs of my boots. Still, I could not help the sheer disappointment at seeing how many were available to the average consumer these days.

I sighed and caught the attention of my new pal.

"What's in yer mind, stranger?" He queried, running stubby fingers through the tangled tumbleweed of his chin.

"Nothing," I said while I peered out of the side window. "A little . . . I don't know, *homesick*, I suppose."

The driver just chortled a bit before replying, "Was gonna ask ya about that accent, where ya from? The States?"

"Something like that," I answered politely as the loco-moti-cart pulled to a stop and the steam whistle of the train hooted loud enough to wake the dead.

We were now in front of a strange building, both in

stature and in architecture. Pipes of various sizes coiled and snaked up its brick exterior, curling past several misshapen windows. Some were square, some more rectangular, however there were also small triangular windows that speckle it as obscurely as stars in the night sky, along with a half dozen oval windows near the building's top half. Two large, mechanical doors sat at the bottom with an exposed gear locking mechanism that whistled a hiss of steam as they opened and shut, but there were several *other* doors that also covered the exterior higher up.

I looked skyward toward them, and mentally questioned how someone would *possibly* get down from a door that high up without a stairway or steam-a-vator system, until an upper door swung for the fences and a jaunty, gangly fellow exited on a small model rotary-cycle and took to the sky.

My head nodded as if to answer its own question, just as someone approached the cart.

"Ms. Graydon, I presume?" The driver spat in a shout through my open window. I did my best to ignore the flecks of spittle now lining my cheek as I eyed the new passenger.

She was a woman roughly my age with a scowl that could melt the locomoti-cart into a puddle of molten brass. Two auburn eyes glared in my direction, and her painted lips pursed in a cocktail equal parts disdain and dissatisfaction. Unlike some of the other stereotypically gendered outfits I've seen, she dressed somewhat differ-

ently adorned in a long jacket of simple beige with orna-
mented leather and copper accents along the lapel and
down the torso. It was a tight fit that fanned out to reveal
black pants and cuffed boots with brass studs at the heel
and tip.

I was just admiring how the golden pins held her hair
up like dazzling rays of the sun, when I noticed her
noticing me. With an astonishing lack of subtlety, I quickly
darted my eyes away.

"Vee," she said and ran her gaze over the cart. Her
voice was elegant yet sharp, her tongue cut each word
precisely as they passed her lips. "Call me Vee."

"Right then, Vee it is." The driver tilted his head and
gave a slight tip of his hat, "The name's Bourbony. Now,
ma'am, might I just ask ya if ya had any drinks this fine
evening?"

I could not help but be a little slighted when the driver
formally introduced himself to this new client without
mentioning his name even once to me, until I remembered that I was *not* a traditional paying client. I let the
thought slip through my mind and fade away.

She glowered at *Bourbony*. "No."

"Then, ma'am, you have the choice of the cart," he said,
presenting the rear with a stretched arm and flat hand
before waving it forward again. "Or the front cabin with
us! Which'll it be?"

I noticed that the driver is using his *paying customer*
tone with her as well which instilled just a tinge of guilt.
The *name* dilemma I could overlook, however it was clear

that Bourbony regarded me as charity work rather than companionship. I will remember to leave him a tip before I make my exit.

Vee rolled her piercing eyes and sucked at the back of her teeth. "My nose may be deceiving me, *Driver*, but I believe I can smell the remnants of regurgitation and urine on your *cart* from here."

She popped open the passenger door to the front cabin as I slid into the middle. It was obvious that there was some expectation that I would vacate my position entirely and relocate to the cart, however I liked the *finders keepers* motto best in situations like these.

Bourbony gave a horizontal scoot as well, opening just a hair of room for me to shuffle more as Vee climbed in. Our trio sat shoulder to shoulder as the door knocked shut and the locomoti-cart scampered down the stones toward Vee's destination.

Now that she was close, I could smell the subterfuge of vanilla and cinnamon wafting from her attire. It was pleasantly pungent enough to falter the scent of rye gin that seemed to crawl from Bourbony's beard yet was not the fancy sort that spoke of evening dates or casual pleasantries. No, if experience served me correctly this young lady was on her merry way to something a bit more professional.

Curiosity got the better of me, yet nativity would be my ally.

"Vee, right?" I asked after several more minutes of silence.

She continued her focus out of the passenger window but replied with a begrudged, *"Yes?"*

"Ah," I remarked. "Big date this evening then? Or just out for a night cap?"

I could tell my accent had her off balance somewhat as she turned her head towards me in an examination. She scoured my clothes, and I could see she paid special attention to the empty orb slots on my gloves; luckily, I removed the Shiver Attunement orbs just before entering the locomoti-cart earlier.

It may have been some years since my last visit to Vangard, but if memory served correctly then any elementally affixed Attunement orb of that size would be immediately seen as hostile. While the size of the vacant slot on the gloves alone may cause curiosity, it did not warrant much suspicion. With the way her eyes lingered on them for just a breath or two, it was obvious that I made the right call.

"Neither," Vee answered pointedly.

"Maybe work then?" I added.

Another eye roll began her response. "Yes, *Statesman*. Work."

Now we were getting somewhere. The way Bourbony shifted uncomfortably in his seat and purposefully avoided the conversation gave away another of Vangard's overbearing laws. Transportation operators could not question clients about their business. Only the location of pick up, the final destination, and then wild assumption filled the space between. Privacy and security in Vangard were top priority, so much so that it choked the last breaths of life from its citizens most of the time.

And yet they wonder why Vangard is ranked first for both military strength *and* alcohol consumption.

"I appreciate you noticing," I said with a smug grin and placed a flat hand over my heart in the known gesture representing the States. "If I may dare to ask . . . " I began and Vee grew tense with gradually blooming annoyance. "What is one so *keen* as yourself doing with a job so late in the midnight hour?"

Now she was the one who shuffled uneasily instead of Bourbony. It was clear the question had thrown her, and now she had a decision to make; Lie to the friendly Statesman or give an ounce of vulnerable truth. I knew her kind well, the ones so closed off to the world that they held a barrier nearly as tall and thick as the stone wall surrounding Vangard. I could appreciate that level of caution, yet I had always found the best path was a combination of both. Shed the barrier just a bit with a small fabrication of the truth then rebuild.

"I am . . . " She paused and glanced at me once more. As if to determine if she would move forward or not. With an exhale she said, "I am one of the head of a specialized task force. Put together by the Wardens to find and capture the *Kugelschurke* once and for all. The bastard . . . " She paused once more and shook her head, her fists clenched on her lap now. "I don't expect a *Statesman* to know about the assailant, but they have been a thorn snuggly plunged in our ribs for some years now."

I cocked a slight grin a bit as she spoke. The Wardens were a branch of law enforcement here in Vansgard that I was all too familiar with, especially after our little chase earlier in the evening. However, *Kugelschurke* was something new. From what I could translate it vaguely came to be *Orb Rogue*. The meaning was simple enough to understand, and something spherical felt just a tad bit heavier within my coat as she spoke more of the thief.

"They came and went without a trace a few years ago. Single handedly raiding an archive housing some of the rarest, and deadliest, Attunement orbs we knew of."

Before she could finish, Bourbon decided to chime in after all. He seemed to perk up a bit as the conversation began to push toward the direction of the *Kugelschurke*.

"Aye. The way a few loose-lipped saucy Wardens explained it back then, it was nothing but a ghost who took down the most heavily guarded area in all of the city." Bourbon grinned and waggled his beard from side to side as he shook his head. "My, what a spectacle that must've been! A bunch of wee Wardens huntin' down some little fella who was armed enough to take down the entire block with a shake of their hands!"

A bellowing tummy laugh echoed from Bourbony's open mouth, and his joy was more than infectious as I joined him. Vee did not seem as pleased with this fond memory, and her scowl deepened while her brow furrowed. Her arms crossed in front of her chest and she huffed in an even greater annoyance.

"*How fun,*" she punctuated in a stern breath. "I do not

imagine our fair chauffeur would be quite so cheery about it if he *really* knew what was at stake. A city block?" She practically scoffed at the thought. "Try Vangard as a whole, or the surrounding towns and territories."

Vee seemed to lean in further, her eyes fixated on one of us before flicking back to another anxiously. Her eyebrows had deepened into a furious gaze, and her nostrils flared in a tauren fury.

"These were no idle trinkets, no minor Attunements of Glow, Gust or Tinder. By the seven Hells, they were not even comparable to the weaponized ones our Wardens utilize such as Scorch or Bolt! These were..." She stopped speaking once more and leaned back into her own seat, eyes falling to stare out the window at the light rain that began to kiss the windows of the locomoti-cart and gloss the cobblestones. "These were mechanisms of war and chaos. Attunements so powerful they were rarely spoken of even in seats of power, so deadly that they could not be documented. The only one I had even heard mild whispers of was known as Heaven's Earth... and even then, only a select few if *any* actually know what it does. And that is just one of the items they stole!"

My heart clunked hard in my chest. The palms of my hands began to perspire and cause the light leathers of my gloves to glue themselves against my flesh. Heaven's Earth was not a phrase I had heard, but I could guess with a name like that what kind of devastation it caused. Did she speak of . . . No, couldn't be. I rattled the thought loose from my skull. Instead, I focused on the here and now.

The world that slowly crept outside of the window, of Vee and her duty to her city, and of Bourbony with his cheery grin. Three souls on individual journey's that I could only hope would not intertwine even further than they already had.

The cart chugged on through the night and silence reigned over us once more.

After prolonged moments, which may have been hours or *days*, the chugging of the locomoti-cart began to grind slower on the stone streets. Before us, a long stretch of similar steam engine vehicles was lined up one after another in a row that seemed never ending as it wrapped a corner. The chorus of toots and whistles broke my concentration enough for me to fully grasp what I was looking at.

My mind had been elsewhere. Carried far from the muggy streets and hissing steam pipes of Vangard, instead focused on what Vee had said for a mild eternity. The orbs. The Attunements taken by *Kugulshurke*. The power she claimed they had and the utter obliteration that Vee and her Warden allies speculated would come at this person's hands. That thought process rattled me, for if this rogue were to utilize them to that dark purpose, then would it not already be so? Why was I the one who could see the forest so clearly through the trees?

When I snapped back to our current reality, it was

clear that something had halted the ground vehicles in their tracks. With a brief glance upward, I was able to deduce that a small force of Wardens hovered above in hydro-thopters forcing any rotary-cyclists to the cobble-stones below as well.

The sight of so many of them gathered and halting traffic made my palms sweat again, and cold perspiration trickled from my neck down my back. I counted seven in the skies from my position, along with three wrapping the turn in the roadway ahead and coming toward us on foot. As the ground units passed, they briefly checked each cart, glancing at a piece of scrap parchment for a moment as they shined orb lights on select individuals. A lump rested firmly in my throat when the thought of the wounded Wardens came to mind, ones who could have easily given a quick description.

Well, shit.

I had hoped to have blended in better for now until the time was right for a flashy retreat. Now, I was sandwiched between a stack of meat driving a locomoti-cart and a specialist of the Warden task force herself. There was no easy way out that would not be anything less than suspicious, and so I let my teeth grind in furious concentration. There just had to be a way out of this!

The orbs felt heavier in the pockets of my overcoat. As if they were the abundant weight of accumulated stress manifested in physics form. They began to feel less like salvation and more like spherical burdens, and my mind raced for a solution to the predicament at hand.

Two vehicles ahead of us, the officers stopped for a longer period of time than they previously had. Many glances to the parchment and back to the person within the vehicle. They looked to each other, one muttered beneath the willow of a groomed mustache while the other gnawed on the end of a fuming pipe. It was then, at the height of my curiosity, that the mustache-adorned officer caught a glimpse of me through the wide front windshield of the locomoti-cart, and I felt the color drain from my body.

"You! You there!" he shouted while his partner seemed to look at where the other pointed. "Remove your gauntlets and exit the vehicle!"

The third Warden was on the other side of a grounded rotary-cycle when the commotion began, and quickly whirled around with a Scorch Attunement orb already equipped to his glove. The other two followed, and soon all three had glowing orange orbs burning just behind their knuckles like campfire embers. Three pairs of furrowed brows and stark gazes fell on our cart, and my hands trembled in their Attunementless gloves.

I looked toward Vee, the specialist of the Warden task force who may just help me from this situation. After all, she had only *just* been called in and would not have witnessed the sketch just yet.

"Vee?!" I practically vomited in anticipation. "They are looking at *us*, why are they looking at us?"

Vee looked to them, then to each of us. Her mind

fitting together pieces of a puzzle that was just a few blocks short of completion.

"You . . . " she said after flicking her eyes from a grinning Bourbony then back to me. "Statesman… it was you! Keep your hands where I can see them!"

Before I could mutter a response, her flintlock was drawn. The single-shot accoutrement that accompanied every Warden of a high rank. Faster than an Attunement but lacking the finesse that these orbs of *magic* seemed to possess. At the visualization of apparent *death,* I raised my gloves upward toward my shoulders.

"Vee, you must *listen—*" I began.

"Enough!" Vee barked. Her eyes shook in fury, the corners of her mouth trembled in a disheartened frown. "You. *You!* You attempt to make me your fool, do you not? Kugelschurke? Smirk at my tales of the *beast* who jeopardizes us all just to remove the masquerade mask and flash your fangs?!"

Vee practically spit as she spoke. Every word laced with acid; every sentence punctuated with the hatred of embarrassment. In a moment of self-reflection I had to wonder if it was merely my presence, or the disappointment of an enemy just beneath her glaring nostrils.

Just the thought of it made my blood run cold when I watched the pistol's barrel reflect the moonlight right before my eyes.

The footsteps of the three Wardens were close. Their boots on the cobblestone were rolling thunderous roars and their shouting continued in mindless circles of *exiting the vehicle* and *putting my hands up*. It was so regulated that I wondered if *they* were powered by the raw steam just as the vehicles and homes. That was until I heard something *change*.

"I repeat, Specialist Vianna Graydon is assisting the target!" One of the three bellowed into a newer model steam-powered phonograph. The copper funnel made the words enhancement tenfold, possible a *hundred*fold, as willows of evaporated fog burst from its opening.

I panicked, but then again it was nothing compared to the pure horrific terror on Vee's face. Her eyes sank, her face loosened, and the realization sprawled over her. The Wardens were practically on the cart, and even Bourbony began to look a little shaken by the utter realization of being caught in the presence of Kugelschurke. An enemy of the government, of Vangard itself! Beside me Vee began to call out to them and explain the situation, but their hardened eyes burned past her excuses and toward their own truth. It was a truth so palpable that I could nearly taste its bitter notes myself.

She was their superior, and this was more of an opportunity for advancement than simply catching the rogue of Vangard.

Bourbony mulled it over as well, and when his hand fell to the ignition rod and began to crank the water-intake I knew our minds were aligned. His foot smashed the pedal, the whistle screamed in puffs of white, moist smoke and the cart lurched forward. It was not quick, but it was *movement* all of the same.

Vee nearly choked from her abrupt inhale and open gasp. Her head cocked to the side, wide eyes staring with raw fury toward Bourbony and myself. The locomoti-cart chugged louder as it gained speed, putting just a bit of distance between the Warden's and ourselves while Vee continued her panicked jolt from us to her peers and back to us again.

"What in the seven bloody Hells are you doing?" she screamed toward Bourbony.

I took as much advantage of the panic as possible and began to rummage inside of my overcoat for the proper Attunements. Something for defense, or rather *offense*, would be first since I expected they would open fire on the cart within the next few seconds. Then perhaps a little something extra as well.

"I'm gettin' us the *seven bloody Hells* outta there, *Specialist Graydon.*" Bourbony mocked back, his eyes remaining implanted on the cobbled road ahead.

The bulky cart pushed as fast as it could, just barely dodging other vehicles while only putting mere feet between us and the Warden's. They ran behind us, boots pattering the stone like successions of heavy rain drops until they found their own vehicles. I could not help but audibly sigh at the realization that we just would not get very far at this rate.

Much to the shock of Vee, and the *awe* of Bourbony, I removed one Shiver orb and placed it into my right Attunement glove. In the left I placed a smoky, emerald green orb that I truly hoped would go unused. Lastly, a translucent orb that seemed to move with a shimmering ripple effect I pulled out from a pocket and held up at eye level.

With piercing eyes, Vee tightened her jaw and raised her flintlock toward me once more.

"You *bastard!*" She bellowed. "I won't let you do this! Stop it now or I will shoot!"

"Vee, listen—"

"I said stop!" Vee interjected. The barrel eyed me carefully.

Unfortunately, her concentration was cut short as a sphere of radiant heat splashed against the cart with a brief wash of flame. The wood paneling took on a dark scorch mark and a scatt of red embers remained burning with a faint glow. The heat from the blast came in the back window, and the three of us ducked a bit instinctively despite no flames actually entering the front cab. Vee let herself look away from me and back toward the quickly gaining Wardens, each already working towards another barrage of fire or lightning.

The area whistle bellowed from the cart as it struggled to push itself faster. Hot water splashed through the pipes to feed the steam engine, and it clinked and clanked as if shouting back that it just could go no faster.

No faster *without* assistance that was.

"I am *not* working with the target! You absolute fools!" Vee screamed back to the Warden trio.

As if to purposefully curdle her blood, the center Warden flashed a grin and punctuated it with a wink. He, and the others, let her know she was heard loud and clear. They just no longer cared for anything other than an open Specialist position in their ranks, along with the capture of the most wanted man in this steaming city.

Me.

Before she could react, I decided to take control of the situation. If there was a deity watching I just hoped they gave me a hint of luck as I opened up the center console control to reveal the water conversion manifold. Bourbony could only gasp in a cocktail blend of confusion and disgust as I plunged one gauntlet to the console, freezing the encasement before smashing it through with the opposite hand. I then gave a brief glance over the inner mechanisms of the engine, which hissed even louder once unshielded and began to exude an intense, humid heat from its bowels. After a moment I found it, the one hidden addition to all steam powered vehicles that rarely went used or noticed at all.

An Attunement Orb slot.

Not so delicately at all, I jammed the misty orb into the slot and watched as it flowed in activation.

"What in the name of-" Bourbony barely began as the engine cranked into overtime and billows of white steam poured from the stack.

The once sluggish locomoti-cart came to new life. Its tires ground deep lacerations in the stones below before finding enough traction to rip forward. An ever-growing distance between us and the Wardens allowed my heart to slow a bit as we watched the blur outside of the windows.

"Ho! Now *this* is power, isn't it?!" The driver chuckled and beamed a wide grin from his beard. "A cart driver can get used to this!"

A crank of a gear, a whisk of the wheel, and the loco-moti-cart banked a turn that was both impossible *and* improbable. It coasted with a roar of steam, the bulk of the cart nearly taking out a row of concerned citizens before sliding to make it around a tall row of buildings. They screamed obscenities of every color toward us, meanwhile the echo of Warden sirens played in the backdrop.

"Take us somewhere safe!" I called to Bourbony over the engine's roar. "Out of *prying* eyes and away from the good people of this city!"

He just passed me that smile as if to say he was having the time of his life. If I was not so worried about my own at the moment, I may have agreed.

"Stop this! Stop this now!" Vee barked with elbows raised to block the spewing heat of the engine.

"A little too late for that I'm afraid," I answered. I jammed a thumb back to point at the space behind us. "We are fast, do not get me wrong. But we are not Warden engineered rotary-cycle fast. They will gain on us if we halt for even a moment."

"And they should! You . . . " Her disdain showed as bright as the steam lights of the city blocks. "You have *ruined* me! You have created chaos yet again!"

Her pistol raised once more and I held my left hand up

in a calming motion, as my right prepared for a rather *cold* defensive strategy.

"I have worked my entire life to stop you . . . to *find* you," Vee said as her pistol trembled. "Our city lives in fear each day for what you may do, for the havoc and devastation you may cause! Do you not understand?"

Her voice faded and became hollow in her next words.

"We know you are here to destroy us . . . "

I took a sharp inhale. A deep one, and it filled my lungs with the moist, warm air of the roaring exposed engine. Her words cut into me, her fearful yet hateful gaze burned me more than the Scorch Attunement orbs ever could. With a moment of silence between us, I lowered my hand and deactivated my Shiver Attunement orb. I returned her look of fear with one of my own.

"That..." I began with regret dripping from my words. "That was never the intention... you must understand that I have never come to harm your people or instill anguish in them. *Fear* in them. Where I come from . . . "

"The States?" She cut in; her pistol still aimed at my temple.

I nodded. "Yes, or rather a version of them. You see, in *my* States we do not possess these orbs. In fact, we possess *very* little of anything. Much of my country and my world has been wiped out by war and famine. And what was left was lost to endless drought before being washed in the endless rain. It was not divinity, or orbs, or magic. It was not fantasy that ruined it all, it was *humanity*. And now I . . . "

I looked behind to see the Wardens regaining their place as they curled around a row of homes behind us.

"I use these orbs, these Attunements, from your world to help save my own." I stated down at the glowing orbs affixed to the back of each gauntlet. "They are *wonderful* tools. They bring fire when we have rain, they bring cold when we have heat. And some . . . well some even bring life where there is only death."

The green orb hummed with its soft luminescent glow on my left hand.

"You can't possibly expect me to believe a single *word* of that," Vee answered. Her eyes lay bewildered by my words and yet somehow transfixed on me at once. "What you imply is not theoretically possibly, *or* probable for that matter. Your claim is . . . "

Before she could finish, a loud hiss rang from the steam stack. The locomoti-cart seemed to lose its impressive speed and began to fall back into its sluggish chug once more. The blur that once was barely recognizable from the windows fell to a creeping image of cobblestones, townhouses, and bending copper pipes that zigzagged from one to the next. A lump found its home in my throat again as I turned back toward the oncoming Wardens.

It was just in time for another sphere of flame to splash over the rear of the cart. A wash of fire sprayed out from the impact, nearly landing within our front carriage.

I had to *do* something.

"Bourbony," I said and turned to the burly driver. "Do you know where we are? Do you know this area well?"

He gave a few nods. Sweat glistened his brow and speckled his coral hued cheeks. I could see the worry set in on him, and just to my other side it spread onto Vee. They both knew they escalated from possibly accomplices to definite allies. My doom would be their own, and their blood would be on my hands.

It was clear. My escape would have to now account for three.

"Alright." I answered as another pepper of fire banked off of the rear cart, followed by a crackle of lightning that chipped segments of the charred wood. "Alright, alright . . . It will have to do. Bourbony," I turned to him once more. "Find is an alleyway in this steam city. Shouldn't be too hard."

"Right," he answered and surveyed the road ahead. "There be a few ahead but they be tight fits for the cart. Otherwise, a larger one would be up a bit yet."

"Small is fine," I practically spat. "Pull the cart up to one, block it off, then make your way down the alleyway. Vee and I will follow you out your door and the two of you will continue down while I hold them back for a moment. Then, we leave."

"What? Absolutely not! I have absolutely, positively *no* interest in leaving with either of you! We must turn ourselves in!"

Vee barely had time to finish her statement by the time our driver found an avenue just large enough for us. The locomoti-cart jerked hard and slammed against a town-house. The bricks and metal screamed as they smeared one another, flakes of wood burst out in a shrapnel flurry and the steam stack let out a high-pitched cry as we slowed down. In our wake there lay a mess of stone and vehicle parts, yet Bourbony lined it up nearly perfect to the alley. Before I could compliment him, another barrage of Attunement orb attacks clattered at the remains of the cart and the large man left his driver's seat to begin down the alley.

I scooted out as well, and as my boots touched the ground I turned back for Vee. Yet, she was frozen.

Not by an orb, but instead by fear itself. It was written on her as it would be a child who was frightened by moving shadows and hidden monsters. I watched her face fall, and it said she knew that all the work of her life had collapsed the moment she met the one person she was tasked with hunting. The one person who gave her life a driving purpose had been the same to rip it all down in a single cart ride late in the evening hour. I cocked my head a bit to the side only to find a few rotary-cycles descending along with the glow of charging Attunement orbs. Either she came, or they would take her out.

Unfortunately, I made her decision for her.

"Come on, Vee!" I shouted and reached out towards her.

I grabbed her wrist with my gloved hand. She was limp as my fingers coiled her, as if she had lost the hope that she would come out of this intact. Still, I did not let her defeat mean *our* deaths. I pulled her close enough where I could comfortably grasp her in both arms and move her from the cart. Her eyes met mine in a flash, her face slowly tightened, and that tough warrior visage came back into the game. Just as her feet touched the stone, she broke from my grasp and began to speed hastily down the corridor of the alleyway.

"Just get us out of this, *Kugelshurke*. Then . . ." Vee said as she made her way forward. "Then you owe me answers."

I gave her a smile and a tip of my head in reassurance. I turned back to see three Wardens closing in from just in front of a burst of steam. The cycles and the cart had been overworked to the point of exhaustion, and it showed in the stiff clouds of white that poured from every grate on them. I stood firm, my eyes meeting theirs while pairs of glowing gauntlets, burning reds and bright electric blue, were affixed on my location. Once a shot was released, I'd be a mount of unrecognizable flesh on the street of Vangard.

I took a breath, then I showed them why I was the legend of their nightmares.

The green glow enveloped me entirely as the left gauntlet grew in power. Just before they released their attack, I slammed my open palm towards the ground and let it ring in a wet *slap* against the moist cobblestone of the steam city. The ground rumbled for just a moment, until a Hell in the tones of rich browns and greens erupted upward. Thick tendrils of plant life burst from the torn stone, lush vines and ivy as thick as tree trunks came forth and sealed the pathway to the alley entirely. The creeping veins of floral power crawled over the townhouses to either side and spread to the rooftops. The power of this orb was incredible, and the longer my hand rested on the ground the more of the city Earth reclaimed.

The Wardens screamed from the other side. Their attacks hit near-harmlessly against the wall of plant life before all I could hear was the sounds of escaping foot-steps and the crunch of powerful vines ripping through stone. I could not be sure behind the wall, but it seemed as though the flora had spread over the entire block within a matter of seconds.

I pulled my hand up, and with a breath of relief I noticed the orb had not been used up entirely yet. Then I turned back to see the horrified gaze of my two newest allies.

"That . . . that . . . " Vee remarked with wide eyes. "That power . . . that was…"

"Yes," I answered with a short nod. "Yes, it was. Heaven's Earth. I was . . . " I turned my head down toward the stone as I walked forward. "I was saving it for something else. But, we are safe for the moment. We have to keep moving before they return with greater numbers."

"Keep movin'?" Bourbony queried and looked around us with a single raised brow. "Bit of a dead end, ain't it?"

I nodded, then removed Heaven's Earth from my gauntlet and placed it into my overcoat. In the same move, I removed something else. Another orb, this one a glowing translucent beauty that gleaned a rainbow prism inside. Their eyes fell on it as I placed it into my gauntlet and let it glow in several shimmering colors at once. Their jaws nearly dropped as I placed the gauntlet on a brick wall beside us and then grunted as the orb grew to a blinding intensity.

"What!" Was all Vee could say as they shielded their eyes with their forearms as the light grew and expanded.

A shrill sound like a hot kettle cracked into the air and a disc of vibrant color slowly encroached over the wall until it was a bit larger than Bourbony. On the other side it was a liquid mirror, but instead of a reflection, it showed a rainbow hovering over water. When they lowered their arms, the beauty of what was before them seemed to nearly knock both to their knees.

"What is this . . . " Bourbony said in a shaking, raspy voice. "It is . . . it is beautiful."

"I do not believe what I am seeing, is that… is that where you are from?" Vee asked as she turned toward me.

I smiled at both, as sirens bloomed once more in the distance and overtook the squeal of the shimmering portal before us.

"It is, and it isn't. My world is . . . " I turned toward the portal myself. "Far from beautiful. But, this will take us there. It will take us to a world without orbs, a world with a different kind of power. I will force neither of you but know that you *will* be safe. And . . . " I gave them both a smile again. "You will be welcomed."

Both inched forward, closing in on the portal. Its

radiant glow spread over them brighter and brighter. Bourbony did not need one more word from me, and before I could even speak he was through the portal. Then, it was just Vee and I. The mortal enemies that neither of us knew about. Her eyes were cold, yet deep within they seemed full of wonder. I reached my other hand out and gestured for her to take it.

She gave one look toward it, another toward the floral colossus, and then placed her hand in mine.

"Alright," she said with new determination. "Let's go. But you still owe me answers."

I chuckled a bit as she moved in the portal, and as it took her in, I followed. As my hand moved inside, the rainbow orb with it, the portal closed behind and warm daylight fell over us. Dry air, soft dirt, and an empty world in need of assistance.

"Trust me, Vee," I said as she scanned her surroundings. "*Now* you will have more questions than I can answer, I am sure."

Nicholas J Evans is an author and musician from Newburgh NY. Prior to his writing debut, he was a co-founding member of the Post-Hardcore group NoraStone as a guitarist. Nicholas appears on their first three studio album: Hopeless Lives & Lullaby's, Sounds Through The Hourglass, and Mortivera.

Order of Dust, his debut novel, was started on late 2017 using the notes section of his iPhone before converting to Google Docs. this is the first novel of his For Humans, For Demons series. In early 2019 the novel series was acquired by The Parliament House Press and released in September of 2020.

Evans currently lives in Maine with his wife and three daughters. He sights inspiration from authors such as:

Neil Gaiman, Alan Moore, Philip K Dick, Yasuhiro Nightow, and Clive Barker.

instagram.com/nickevanswrites

facebook.com/nickevanssaid

twitter.com/nickevanswrites

GOSSAMER & THORNS
BY ELLE BEAUMONT

ONE

"I've almost done it," Dr. Sevrein murmured. He pinched the bridge of his nose and wiped the sweat from his brow with his kerchief, which he then promptly stuffed back into his shirt pocket. Dropping his hand, he muttered and undid the buttons on his high-collared shirt. Eventually, his crystalline gaze slid to the young man at his side.

Kristoph—Kris—stood by his father and frowned, unsure of what to say. What his father was attempting to do was not only taboo, but it was blasphemous to boot. Infusing a human's soul into an automaton was playing God—but who was he to speak out against his father?

What was the point, Kris wondered, of having a human soul trapped inside a machine? They already piloted dirigibles and trains, and cleaned and tended to homes. It was only a matter of time before humans were overrun by automatons. However, Kris's father was a man obsessed with creation, especially if there were any mechanics involved.

Dr. Magnus Sevrein had inherited an earldom when his elderly father had passed, but tending to such responsibilities had never been high on his list of things to do. Instead, he hurled himself into academics and, later on, science. His younger brother, Hakon, stepped in to secure the holdings and the earldom flourished in his care.

When Kris's father married, it was to a woman who sought to climb societal ladders, and Kristoph was born some odd years later. By the grace of all that was good, he was largely raised by the nanny and ignored by his parents. Until he turned thirteen years of age.

His father had drilled into his mind the importance of a good pedigree and what it meant. Good breeding would produce better breeding—as if they were all just prized show ponies. *Good breeding means that genes are protected from Ironbark disease.* A notable disease that swept through Agderland, marking the affected ones with mismatched eyes, a weakened immune system, and inevitably a shortened lifespan. In the worst cases, the patient's body attacked itself and shut down organs, even in the youths.

It amused Kris that his father had never cared so much about legacies outside of beakers, petri dishes, and tinctures. Yet here he was, impressing the importance of smart pairings because Hakon had no son to pass the family estate to, which meant it would go to Kris.

A hiss of a curse emitted from Magnus and a fist collided with the work desk, sending a dish scattering to the floor. "Dammit." His fingers jammed through his faded blond hair. "Get out of here, I have to think. The formula for the binding liquid is off—I have to . . . " His voice trailed off and Kris knew he wouldn't finish.

Reaching into his pocket, Kris pulled out a watch and smiled down at it. It ticked away until the big hand and the little hand pointed to the twelve. In the hallway, the grandfather clock chimed, and with a grin, Kris jogged down the hall, mindful to tiptoe past his mother's room. Most days she didn't bother leaving her room. Her nerves wouldn't allow it and she took to nursing them with a good helping of belladonna. It was something he had grown used to. His parents had never been present in his life.

Quickly descending the spiral staircase, Kris made his way to the front hall and opened the door. A pair of mismatched eyes met his gaze, signifying Ironbark disease. They were the most expressive set he had ever seen: crystal-blue and amber, set in the rounded features of a pale face. Blond hair was held in a tidy chignon, but a few curls framed the doll-like face.

She wore a navy dress jacket, which had ruffles on its high neck. The cut of it tapered in toward her ribs, accentuating her slender figure, and the skirt she wore only came to her knees, allowing Kris to appreciate her legs. They weren't bare, for she wore a pair of brown tights, but he longed to do away with every speck of clothing on her. He'd respected her wishes and remained deferential, but damn if he couldn't help it when his mind wandered.

A slow smile replaced his grin as he swung the door open. "Emilie, I've been waiting for you," he crooned, waving her inside.

At nineteen years of age, Kris should've been in search

of a mistress, or potentially a wife, but he'd never played by the rules. He'd certainly spent a fair amount of time entangled with young ladies, but there had always been one in particular who caused his heart to stutter and his world to slow.

Emilie.

Emilie was only seventeen and her father hadn't been keen on the idea of an engagement before eighteen. Kris could wait six months. What could possibly change in a short amount of time?

"Really?" She wrinkled her pert nose and flashed a brilliant smile at him. "I couldn't tell."

He cleared his throat, casting his eyes toward the ceiling as he feigned embarrassment. Offering his arm to her, Kris allowed her to loop hers through his. "It's been—oh, confound it—a whole four days without seeing you?" He shook his head and grinned as they walked toward the solarium.

Emilie's face lit up as they crossed the threshold. And once they were inside the room, she moved toward a table that held a single plant. She held her hands up as if she were cupping the fragile petals, but she didn't actually touch them. "How is my beautiful Pearl today?"

The Moth Orchid, as it was commonly known, less commonly known as Phalaenopsis Blume, was a vibrant hue of orange with veins of pink streaking across each silken petal. In the center a stark white was seen, and it was why Emilie named the plant Pearl.

Kris shook his head and stuck a hand in his pocket.

The way she named each plant amused him, but what tickled him more was the fact that after she named it the blasted thing seemed to grow and flourish. Of course, there was a scientific reason behind it, which had little to do with a name and everything to do with carbon dioxide. Kris's father had declared that believing a name brought forth life was just hogwash. It may have been, but it warmed his heart to know Emilie loved his plants as much as he did.

"I am certain she's better now that you're here." He sighed heavily, narrowing his eyes on the plant. "She prefers your company."

"Pearl or you?" she teased him.

Moving closer to her, Kris tilted his head to catch her eye. "Me," he said, unabashedly. "I am better now that you're here." There was no point in hiding how he felt about her anymore. They were not children cast aside at a party—they were not young teens withholding laughter at an opera. They were young adults on the brink of something else, something new and exciting.

"Kris," Emilie said softly and dropped her hands, breaking the moment between them. "I have an invitation for you." She pulled her gloves free of her delicate hands and reached into her reticule. "It is six months out, so I assume you'll be able to clear your schedule."

Kris took up the invitation. Cream paper with gold lettering. Blasted thing, stealing the moment. He smiled and read it out loud. "You are cordially invited to celebrate Lady Emilie Nilsson's eighteenth birthday . . . " He paused and lowered the card only a fraction, just his eyes peering over the paper card. "You assume wrong."

Despite the glee that shone on her face, something flickered, perhaps doubt.

"I have nothing planned at all, and would be more than happy to be the first to arrive at your birthday party." He took one of her bare hands in his, felt the softness of her skin against his hands, and bowed his head to brush a kiss against her knuckles.

Emilie gasped softly, then she pulled her hand away only to remove the bonnet on her head. She watched him, color rushing into her cheeks, and Kris wished he could read her mind. "I cannot wait then. Help me tend to these beauties."

Again, Emilie navigated through the tension and pulled away. All Kris longed to do was bury his fingers in her hair, taste her lips, and proclaim his heart belonged to her . . . always.

An hour passed between entering the room and finishing their task of grooming the flowers. It was a tedious thing that the staff wasn't allowed to do, per Kris's instructions. Emilie enjoyed it, and it was fairly relaxing.

"I have a gift for you," Kris said and circled his finger to tell Emilie to spin around. "It took me a while to find it, but I think you'll be rather fond of this." He moved to the potting bench and pulled the fabric away from a covered plant. He smiled down at the strange beauty and looked to Emilie. "You may look now."

Emilie spun around and gasped as she took in the sight of the beautiful flower. It was strange looking; its petals were such a faint purple that it almost looked silver, and the dark purple veins in it made it that much more peculiar. The underside of it retained the same dark hue, giving the flower a steel-like appearance before it bloomed.

"Kris! This is . . . it's the most stunning flower I've seen," she stated softly. Without hesitation, she lifted herself on the balls of her feet and kissed the corner of his mouth.

Stunned but for a moment, Kris froze and wanted nothing more than to dip his head to turn the kiss into something more than chaste and friendly. As Emilie withdrew, a slow rakish grin tugged at his lips. "I know. I searched far and wide for one that would ensure I received a kiss."

"Kristoph Anders Sevrein," Emilie whispered, her eyes playfully narrowing as she chastised him.

Lifting his hands, he turned his attention to the plant again. "Apparently, the flower's creation was quite a task. One of the rarest hybrids out there right now."

"But, where or how did you find it?" Emilie's mismatched gaze widened.

"I have my ways." He rapped a knuckle against the pot and lifted his brows. "Take it home so that you can care for it. I have the instructions here. Along with the difficulty in creating it . . . it seems it's as finicky as the orchids." His eyes focused on her features, and he committed this moment to his memory. The soft blush painting her cheeks. Her full lips parting and begging for him to kiss them. And the sweet innocence swirling within her gaze.

A simple but weighted moment.

Outside in the hallway, the clock chimed the telltale sign of a new hour, and Magnus appeared in the doorway to the room, lifting a disinterested brow in Emilie's direction. "Your mother is requesting your presence, Kristoph. See that your guest finds her way out properly."

Kris's icy gaze flicked toward his father. It was no secret that his father thought very little of the Nilsson family and hadn't the decency to even show the tiniest bit of courtesy to them. They were beyond inferior in his eyes, for Ironbark disease ran in their family. Of course, Emilie never thought ill of Kris.

As soon as his father slid from the doorway, he lowered his gaze. "I'm sorry," he murmured, blond hair tumbling into his eyes.

"You are not your father, Kristoph. Never forget that." She lifted a hand, brushing the strands of hair from his face. "I'll see myself out. Thank you for the gift." Emilie took a step forward and this time she brazenly pressed her lips against Kris's. "Until tomorrow."

The breath escaped Kris and he watched, dumbfounded, as Emilie walked out of the room. *Why did*

Mother have to ruin this moment? Grinding his teeth, he stormed out of the room and back up the spiral staircase.

The door to his mother's room was open just a crack, and Kris wished nothing more than to flee down the hall to the privacy of his room, but alas, he had been called. He pushed inside, and the light filtered into the otherwise darkened room. His mother sat with her head propped against an array of pillows and if it hadn't been for her eyes, which were blankly staring at a spot across the room, he'd have thought her to be asleep. When Kris shifted, her eyes locked onto his.

Perhaps if he didn't move, she wouldn't see him—it was something he'd thought as a child, and sometimes it worked back then. No such luck would allow that to happen. Not as her hand swept away strands of hair from her brow, not as she scooted into a sitting position and the down blanket slid from her and revealed her ivory nightdress.

"Come sit with me, my son." She patted the bed next to her, clearly still groggy from the effects of the drug.

His feet felt weighed down as if by lead. But dutifully, Kristoph moved toward the bed and sat. "What is it, Mother?" His words were clipped.

"Can't a mother ask to visit with her son? Honestly, one would think you didn't love me at all."

He didn't. At least he was fairly certain he didn't. She had been largely absent from his life, far too busy playing hostess and occupied with staying relevant in society to pay any mind to him unless it was to parade him around like a doll. And as much as he loathed to admit it, his father had been more of an influence than she had. His mother also had a tendency to lash out and cut him down, which had hardened his heart toward her over the years.

The silence seemed to infuriate her. She curled her lip as she looked up at her son. "You act as though you are ill-bred, and we know that isn't true."

His father wasn't the only one who impressed the importance of breeding, but his darling mother wasn't strong, not like him and not like his father. She was a prisoner to the vial next to her bed and the nerves that drove her to it.

"Pardon me, but what do the ill-bred act like, Mother? You act as if they're another breed entirely." He pressed his lips into a firm line and simply waited for whatever insults she was surely about to sling his way, if she could even muster them.

"I'd prefer you find a suitable girl. Your father said that the Nilsson girl was here. You know what you'll be inheriting, so aim higher than that diseased thing." His mother and father shared the same views on strength and preserving genetics. Since Emilie was born with Ironbark, neither one of his parents viewed her as anything more than a genetic tragedy.

Red bled into Kris's vision as anger blossomed in his chest and spread throughout his body. That was enough. Insulting him was one thing, but dragging Emilie into it? He stood up and shot her a glare. "Bite your tongue, woman. Your opinion means very little to me when it comes to strength. You cannot pry yourself from bed long enough to even bathe properly, so please spare me your judgment of what strength is." He sneered and began to walk away. "We are done here."

His mother gasped as if someone had slapped her, then her gray eyes grew as cold as steel. "You will never find happiness with her, Kristoph. Never." Her lips twisted into a humorless smile, and her frame fell against the mound of pillows. She laughed tiredly, but it sounded sinister just the same and it chilled him to the core.

A loud bang, followed by the vibration of the doorjamb, startled Kris awake. His mussed hair hung in his vision, obscuring the figure standing in his doorway. But as the heavy, quick steps traveled across the floor, he knew who it was. Father.

"Get up." His father pried the down blankets from him. "Get up now. You need to help me figure this out." His voice was tight with barely restrained fury and Kris could hear the madness, too.

"What the hell time is it?" Kris croaked. A warm glow peeked through the drapes, which meant it was after seven in the morning.

Magnus Sevrein's obsession with science always drove him to madness, especially when he couldn't figure out a problem. Unfortunately for Kris, his father would drag him into it, leaving him no option but to learn the art of alchemy, when all he wanted was to study botany.

Knowing better than to argue when his father was in such a state, Kris rolled out of bed. "Can I get dressed, at least?"

His father blinked owlishly, then, as he realized his son was in his night clothes, he nodded. "Be quick and meet me in the cellar." With the words barely off his lips, he left the room.

Quickly, Kris pulled on his trousers and a white linen button up. Over that, he wore a cerulean vest with a white paisley print on it. Once he slid his feet into his calf skin button boots, he was out the door and rushing down to the cellar, lest he deal with another tirade from his father.

The cellar was damp, as was expected, but it didn't lack lighting. It was far too bright, in Kris's opinion. Bronze gas-lamps dotted along the walls, and where there wasn't a shelf lined with bottles, gears, or some kind of tool, they cast a golden glow to the entire room. From the ceiling hung several sprawling chandeliers, each boasting a lit candle.

In the middle of it all, hung suspended by chains, a nondescript automaton stared lifelessly at the stone floor. Bronze limbs hung limp at its sides, and the smooth column of a neck tilted at the base at an unnatural angle.

It wasn't as if the machines were uncommon in Agderland, so Kris wasn't startled to see it. Several machines worked in their family home. Automatons were immortal in the sense that they were machines and couldn't die. It was far easier to replace a part than it was to replace a human. So many households employed them, and so many businesses were overrun with them too.

Kris had seen far more detailed machines before, with hair and grafted skin pulled over titanium limbs. But the quality of the machine had little to do with the success of infusing a human's soul with one and everything to do with the process and formulation. It was tedious work, but done slowly and efficiently, it was possible. Dr. Rolf Yotun had accomplished it in his last years alive. He'd even boasted of his accomplishment, hiding away his notes. But his automaton turned on him, so it was assumed, for Dr. Yotun's body was discovered outside of his home, his heart ripped from his chest. But his notes were lost when the machine set fire to his home, destroying everything, including his creation.

"Are you just going to stand there?" his father snapped, narrowing his eyes at Kris who stood at ease near the door.

"I might," Kris muttered under his breath, pushing off the wall. He crossed the room and stood at the work-bench, plucking up a notebook. He pored over the text, and his eyes slanted toward the automaton then toward the silver table beside it. On the slab, a man lay shivering. "Father . . ." He froze, clutching the notebook tightly.

Kris had never killed a thing in his life and if his father thought he'd partake in extracting the man's soul, he was sadly mistaken.

His chest grew heavy as reality settled in. How had his father gotten this man here? Pressing his lips together, Kris withheld a cry of disgust and stamped it down enough for it to be a grunt. However, his eyes grew blurry with tears of fury and revulsion.

"Don't fuss so." His father waved him off as he bent over the man. The man's sickly skin already had a gray tone to it, as if someone had drained the blood from his body. And perhaps someone had. "This is Trevor Absen. He's dying and wishes to give his body to science." His tone implied that he was doing the good man's will. Kris felt like vomiting.

Distracting himself by looking down at the notebook, Kris noted that blood had in fact been taken from the man and bound to an alchemical agent that, when pumped through the automaton, should bind and infuse the machine with the man's soul.

Blood possessed memories, which made sense. It was with a being nearly since conception. Memories were consciousness, but what of the soul? Did it run through the veins as well?

"This will ease the pain." Magnus slid a thin white tablet beneath the dying man's tongue and observed him. "Thank you," he murmured so lowly that Kris could barely hear him, "for giving yourself to science." Then he scooped a scalpel up and dragged the tip across Trevor's wrist. A ribbon of red appeared, rushing down the man's palm then fingertips before finally draining into an awaiting pail.

Kris looked away, but the smell of the blood threatened to make him ill.

"I woke you so you could help me, not so you could stand and gawk at the floor." Waving the bloody scalpel, his father motioned to the brown liquid on the counter.

"Take the blood and pour it into that mixture. Don't spill it; it's the life force that will bring the automaton to life."

Kris glanced around the table, found a pair of gloves, and tugged them on. Obediently, he took the pail of blood and replaced it with another pail before he returned to the workspace where the mixture awaited. With a furrowed brow, he poured it into the tall beaker. The blood roiled at the fresh addition, then settled.

"Good," his father said from behind him. "Begin pouring it into the machine."

Kris looked over his shoulder, a question on his lips as to where to pour it, but he could see a funnel with a long tube traveling into the automaton's back. Carrying the mixture over, he poured it into the funnel. The dark liquid zigzagged through the rubber hose until it settled into the awaiting drum inside.

"The key is to infuse live blood with the compound I created. The compound will fuse to the life force in the blood." Magnus paused, clucking his tongue as he noticed Trevor had passed on. He pulled a sheet up over the man, then shifted his attention toward the machine. He flicked his blood-covered fingers at a panel on the front of the automaton, bringing forth a clicking-whir sound from it.

Kris stumbled back and quickly deposited the tall beaker on the table. He didn't want to be next to whatever abomination was about to spring to life. In jerky movements, the machine twisted its head, arms, and legs, as if testing them out. Dread unfurled in Kris's stomach. What had his father done?

"Yes!" his father bellowed, thrusting a triumphant fist into the air. "I've done it."

But just as quickly as the words had left his mouth, the automaton spasmed. Limbs twisted in on themselves, its head cocked back, and a groaning, human sound escaped the machine, which swiftly turned into a ghastly cry.

Smoke billowed from the creature, then it ceased all movements. Black liquid seeped from the automaton's mouth, looking eerily like blood.

Kris had never heard something so terrifying before. Like a man's dying wail, fused with a banshee's howl.

"What have you done?" His father's voice took on the sharpness of accusation. His pale features turned red as he turned on Kris, fingers curling into a fist.

"M-me?" If he hadn't been half distracted by the horrifying display, Kris would have bolted out the door. As his father's fist connected with his cheek, he fell against the table. Tears burned in his eyes against his wishes—not because he was hurt, but because frustration bubbled within.

If Kris's father had his wits about him, he'd know it wasn't his son's fault, but when Kris chanced a look at him, he knew his father's mind was gone. His eyes were wide, lips pinched in fury. He wasn't *there*. Kris had experienced his father's crazed behavior far more times than he cared to admit. And his physical wrath wasn't anything new either; although as he'd grown older, taller, his father hit him less.

Instead of sticking around, he bolted from the basement, ignoring the howls of displeasure from his father and the slurs that escaped him. He ran as fast as he could up the hall and out of the manor. Tension tightened every one of his muscles. Gone was the heartbreak that swiftly ensued after being struck, and in its place was a hardness, a growing cool indifference to everything about his father.

A footman huffed and twirled on his heel. "Sir, would you—"

"No!" Kris didn't bother to stick around. His feet and long legs carried him through the courtyard and onto the drive, and before long he was running down the cobblestone road toward Emilie's house.

Sweat trickled down his brow and stung his cheek. He lifted a hand, swiping at it only to find blood on his fingertips. Frowning, he shoved the images of the dead man on the table and the writhing automaton from his mind.

Blinded temporarily by his sweat, Kris failed to see a gnarled root on the side of the road. He tripped on it, which sent him sailing forward. He caught himself, hands taking the brunt of the force, but it jarred his shoulders.

Sucking in a ragged breath, he squeezed his eyes shut and refused to think of the horror in his basement.

"Kris, oh my lord, are you all right?" A familiar, soft voice carried to him, but he was focusing on ignoring the flashing images in his mind haunting him. "Kristoph!" Emilie's tone grew panicked when he didn't respond.

He opened his eyes as gentle, gloved fingers probed along his jawline. A soft gasp came from her when she tilted his head up and met his eyes. No doubt the mark on his cheek inspired the look of shock on her face. Without a mirror, he couldn't know how unsightly it was or wasn't. "I'm fine." Kris averted his gaze, clenching his jaw as he buried his feelings deep within.

"No, you're not." She knelt in front of him, shaking her head. "Let's get you into the house and cleaned up. You can tell me what happened . . . if you want to."

In the house? Kris blinked. Confusion rumpled his brow and tilted his lips. When he surveyed the area, he saw the Nilssons' pale yellow house with a red roof. On the wraparound porch, he could make out Emilie's parents, who presently stood at the railing, brows lowered and confusion rumpling their expressions as if they were concerned.

The black iron gate whined as a gust of wind caught it and pulled it open, as if it wished for him to step through too.

"I didn't realize . . . " His words trailed off as Emilie's fingers dragged along his cheek to his jawline and into his hair. Kris's eyes fluttered closed, lulled by the tender, soothing touch. A stark contrast from the punch his father had delivered.

If he could stay in that moment he would have, but they were in the middle of the road, and even Emilie's patient parents would hardly enjoy their daughter making a spectacle of herself.

"Come with me," Emilie prompted again.

And that was all the prompting he needed.

Kris stood, dusting himself off. He'd torn a hole in his slacks and blood stained his linen shirt.

Emilie slid her arm through his and pulled him through the iron gate. "There is still some breakfast out if you—"

"I would love that." He leaned into her, dipping his head down to run the tip of his nose along her ear. "Thank you."

THREE

Indoors, Emilie led Kris to the sitting room and ran to fetch the first aid kit. An amber bottle with a stained orange-brown cap sat on a dark oak table. Instead of wallpaper, the walls were painted ivory with gold trim, and the far side was painted a deep maroon.

Although it was a stark contrast to the cellar of his family home, the smell of the iodine brought back the dying man's face. Kris grimaced at the intrusive image, wanting nothing more than to blot it away.

When had his father become so sordid? And if his father's blood coursed through him, did that mean Kris would inevitably become just as cold as he was?

"Let me see that," Emilie murmured, dabbing some of the orange liquid onto a cloth. She blotted it along his cheekbone, which pulled a hiss of pain from Kris. "I'm sorry."

"Don't be. It isn't your fault." Kris lifted his hand, his fingers lighting on her wrist. He wanted so badly to tell her why he'd run blindly and fell. But could he? It was known his father wasn't of the soundest disposition.

Magnus would throw tantrums if his research didn't go accordingly, and that hadn't changed as long as Kris had been alive.

Emilie's mismatched eyes studied him. She licked her full lips, then cast her glance to the floor. "I want more for you, Kristoph. More than your life with your parents. You know that."

"If I could escape—if we could—I'd run and never look back. The only thing keeping me here is you." Kris caught Emilie's wrist, then brought her hand up so he could brush featherlight kisses against her knuckles.

She sucked in a breath but didn't pull her hand away. Kris placed it against his chest so she could feel the steady thrumming of his heart.

"I would . . ."

There was a *but* that hung heavily between them. He longed for Emilie to continue what it was she was on the verge of saying, but the scuffling of feet outside the room brought his attention away from Emilie's cherubic face. He offered a tight smile to Emilie's mother as she rushed up to the couch he sat on.

Emilie had the same full face as her mother, but where her daughter possessed Ironbark's mark of mismatched eyes, she had a matching pair of blue ones. Despite the fact that she was middle-aged, her skin shone with youth and her blond hair held on to its luster. She frowned, eyes searching his face. "You poor thing. Was this done by—"

"Yes." Kris didn't see a point in lying. The Nilssons weren't unaware of who his parents were or what sort they were. They'd seen a fair share of bruises on his face and arms over the years. "I'm all right."

"I'm sure you are, but Kristoph, you can stay here tonight if you wish. We have the spare room open, and it would allow for things to simmer down." Her voice trailed off, a hint of hopelessness in her tone.

With the windows open, the whistle of the steam engine rolling into the center of town was loud. The ten o'clock engine had arrived and would transport citizens out of Agderland and toward the Vitblek Mountains in the distance and beyond.

Beyond, Kris thought, what a wonderful thing that would be as long as Emilie was by his side.

He caught a look of uncertainty in Mrs. Nilsson's gaze. "I appreciate that, but it isn't necessary." Tentatively, Kris reached out and took a hold of her hand, squeezing it. "Truly. My father will be distraught and holed up in his room now. I won't see either of my parents once I venture home."

"At the very least, you must stay for supper."

A small laugh escaped Kris. "I will take you up on that offer." He followed Mrs. Nilsson's movements as she glided along the floor.

"I'll let the cook know." She offered him a small smile, then left Emilie and Kris alone.

"It's hard to believe that we met quite by accident." He shifted on the couch, making room for Emilie to join him. She sat down, arranging her petticoat and skirt. She leaned into the corner of the couch, smiling at him. "If I hadn't been cross with my mother, I'd never have stumbled on you sobbing over a lost ribbon."

Emilie had been a wreck when he stumbled on her when she was only twelve. Although he couldn't understand why she'd been fussing over a ribbon, Kris had empathized with her distress and he'd helped her find it.

Emilie had looked at him as if he were some hero, when all he'd done was pull the pastel green ribbon from a bush. Little did he know it had belonged to her late grandmother, and the ribbon held fond memories of their time shared; it was only a ribbon to him, but it meant so much more to the little girl.

"It wasn't about the ribbon!" Emilie hissed, thwapping his arm playfully. "It was about who gifted the ribbon to me."

"Oh yes, yes . . . " He lifted a hand and pressed a finger to his lips in thought, but as he glanced down, he saw flecks of blood. Blood that wasn't necessarily his. Kris blanched, his head drooping. "I wish we could go back to then."

"I don't," Emilie was quick to say, "because I'd have to wait that much longer to spend the rest of my days with you."

Warmth spread through Kris at her words. In the past years, both he and Emilie hinted at deeper feelings, but neither one confessed their feelings to one another. But Kris knew he loved Emilie and knew every time he gazed into her eyes she felt the same way, too. It was in the subtle touches, the way her voice went up an octave when they were in one another's company, and how she encouraged him to be more than a product of his upbringing.

They were more. Weren't they?

"I'm . . . I'm more than an escape, aren't I?" he whispered. Vulnerability was an ugly thing in his family, but Kris couldn't stop his lips from moving.

Emilie's eyes widened. She quickly leaned forward and grabbed both of his hands in hers. Pain entered her gaze, but then her brows lifted. "Kristoph, you are everything I could ever hope for."

She was holding back still. He could hear it in her tone and as he searched her eyes, there was something there, too. "Emilie," he whispered, and pulled one of his hands free. He tucked the tendrils of blond behind her ear. "You are my heart and I love you." The confession spilled out, but he couldn't stop. "Without you, I'd cease. A shell would be left behind, with no soul."

Emilie sucked a breath in, then leaned closer to him. A blush entered her cheeks, and she exhaled shakily. "I love you and have loved you ever since you pulled my ribbon free from the rosebush." She squeezed his hand, glanced over her shoulder quickly, and turned back to him. Without hesitating, her lips clashed with his, unpracticed and innocent.

But heaven help him . . . between the sweet perfume that clung to her and the taste of her mouth against his, Kris wished her parents weren't home. He cupped her cheek, tilting Emilie's head for better access. His tongue swiped along hers, pulling a groan from him. If he could grab her by the hips and pull her on top . . .

Kris interrupted his thoughts and withdrew from her. "I want to, but your parents . . . " He eyed the doorway as if they'd walk in at any moment, and they might have.

Emilie's cheeks burned with desire and it reflected in her eyes, which only added to his discomfort.

One day, she'd be his entirely. Until then, he had to wait.

Emilie lifted her hand and the pad of her thumb dragged along his cheekbone. "You are a good man, Kristoph." She tilted her head, following his gaze as he shifted it away. "Your heart is in the right place all the time."

If Kris could absorb Emilie's purity, he would have. But it would have to be enough to bask in her presence. Her gentleness always seemed to soothe the shadows that lurked within his mind. The same demons that threatened to spread, much like a virus, through him. The older he became, the more he felt the taint of them.

He leaned forward, closing the gap between them, and pressed his lips to hers once again. He savored the taste of her honey lips, allowing her light to spread through him. "Of all the things I've stumbled on in my life, you are by far my greatest find."

"Miss Emilie," a tinny voice called from the doorway. A sleek automaton shifted its position. Then, with a tilt of the head, it walked into the room, far more agile than it should've been. It wasn't a model that boasted humanoid aspects outside of the shape of its body. "For the sake of propriety, please remain at least six inches away from Lord Sevrein at all times." Amber eyes stared at Kris and Emilie like two golden lamps. No skin covered the automaton, no hair. It was just metal.

Kris withdrew from Emilie, his eyes following the machine. At once, Trevor's face floated to the forefront of his mind and his stomach lurched.

Despite the conflict rising within, Kris managed a smile when Emilie huffed.

Emilie twisted and cast a narrowed glance at the automaton. "Moddy, did Mother send you?" In reply, the machine remained silent and still. "Moddy."

Kris leaned against the couch, chuckling to himself. "You know your mother did." Not that he could blame her for sending a machine in to disturb them. But he still didn't appreciate the interruption.

Moddy's neck whirred as she glanced from Emilie to Kris. "That is correct, young Lord. Miss Nilsson knows it isn't proper for—"

"Oh! Very well." Emilie sprung to her feet and twirled to face him. "Now that we have a chaperone, I suppose we should take advantage of the sun and take a walk." She looked at him through her thick blond lashes and smiled shyly. "If you wanted to stay for supper, that is . . ."

"On both accounts, I'd love to." He stood, offering his arm to Emilie despite the repetitive lecture Moddy hummed. "It would be entirely remiss of me to not offer the young lady an arm. And while you're there, Moddy, surely I cannot be a rascal."

Twin lights peered at him, fading for a moment then lighting back up. The automaton seemed to process what he said, for she stepped back and allowed Kris to lead Emilie out of the room. But Moddy's footfalls were less than stealthy. The machine clopped on the wooden floor as heavily as a horse might.

Emilie locked eyes with Kris. She sighed, leaning into him, and although they weren't alone, unable to explore one another, it was enough for him.

For hours, Kris strolled the streets of Skonstad city with Emilie and clunky Moddy. It had been the only home he knew. A beautiful cityscape set beside the Blatt Sea, with spires that stretched toward the sky and plumes of steam that puffed from the factories, as well as roaring engines.

The cobblestone streets boasted a slick sheen from the humid air. Even amidst mountains, the warm summer sun wasn't enough to chase away the chill that swept through in the night.

Kris didn't want to move away from Skonstad. But if it meant a happy life with Emilie, he'd do anything he could.

# FOUR

A few days after the failure of binding the soul to the automaton, Kris's father was back to speaking to him. Not that Kris had any desire for it.

How could someone kill another and feel nothing? His father blathered on about the technicalities of the science behind it. That he was still missing one thing, and that was enough to send it all off course.

That was all he cared for, and it should have surprised Kris but it didn't.

"Kristoph," his father called down the hall from the solarium.

If he could have turned into the plant he was tending, Kris would have taken the moment to do just that. But his father slid into the solarium, pale-blue eyes bright and his cheeks flushed. If Kris didn't know any better, he'd think his father was drunk, but he was only frenzied with inspiration or discovery.

"I need you to look over these notes with me." His father waved the papers around then paused in the doorway. His lips pressed into a thin line as he regarded the plants Kris tended to. "You can play with your things later."

Things, he thought bitterly. The *things* his father disregarded were highly sought-after plants, and some were even hybrids Kris had created over the years. No, he didn't toil with rivets, cogs, or gears. He preferred botany above all else.

Over the years, Kris had developed a thick skin when dealing with his father. His words plinked against the armor he'd constructed in his presence, tumbling down to the dirty floor. "Let me see them." He lifted a brow, casting his father a dry glance.

"These aren't them," his father snapped. "These are the errors I've found."

It was difficult to withhold a sneer of his own and brush his father off, but Kris did.

With a sigh, he placed the potted orchid onto the table. Aside from turning to face his father, he hadn't actually made any movements toward him. Glancing down, he picked up a bronze watering can and spritzed a few of the unhappy blooms.

An impatient exhale prompted him to set it back down. He smiled as he rolled up his sleeves and walked up to his father. "What do you need help with exactly?"

When Magnus Sevrein grew cross, his brows furrowed, his lips pinched together, and his eyes looked as if they'd freeze over a room. He looked very much like that, and Kris's amusement mounted. It wasn't every day he could rouse a reaction from his father.

"My notes," he bit out, rubbing the wrinkle between his eyebrows. "Something is amiss. And . . . I need another set of eyes. You've helped me for years. Surely you can spot something?"

"Maybe." Kris shrugged. "But I also have no schooling in Thanatology or reanimation." His expertise didn't lie within the realm of the dead or bringing them back to life. Sighing, Kris looked to the skylights above. The trailing ivy snaked along the iron bars crafted specifically for them, and the palm trees stretched toward the sun's bright rays. His solarium looked more akin to a jungle than a room set off to the side of their home.

His father pinched the bridge of his nose, as if gathering his patience thread by thread. "I just need your eyes, Kristoph."

"So you've said." Kris kept his tone light, even though he felt anything but. Snatching up a cloth, he wiped the dirt from his hands then shoved it into his back pocket before following his father out into the hall.

Upstairs, the sound of glass shattering echoed through the halls, accompanied by a shrill scream. His mother likely ran out of her belladonna, or had been rationing it, because their family physician refused to give it to her any longer.

Muffled voices—the servants'—joined the wailing, pleading with her.

"She isn't feeling her best today, your mother."

His father was keen on making excuses for her, but Kris's well had run dry of them. There were no excuses for either of his parents. He also didn't care whether she felt well. When did she ever think to ask him how he felt?

Down the hall, toward the cellar door, Kris caught a whiff of the chemicals his father used. It burned his nose and smelled of rotten eggs. Nothing in him wished to go down the stone stairs. The memory of the dead man was far too fresh in his mind.

He gritted his teeth as he lingered at the top, but his father's impatient sigh drew Kris down the steps. Couldn't his father have snagged the notes from his work desk and handed them over? Did Kris *have* to venture down—

"Would you cease dragging your feet?"

Behind him, Kris rolled his eyes but hurried down after his father. Did he want to quicken his strides? No, but the sooner he glanced at the notes, the sooner he could run back up the stairs. And as he stepped onto the cellar floor, his eyes immediately went to where the man had died. He was long since gone, but Kris could almost see his body again.

His father rummaged on the desk, pulling Kris's attention away from the table. "What is missing?" He thrust the notebook at him, features as tight as his voice was.

Quietly, Kris flipped through the pages. The script was so familiar, as were the notes. He read over what his father had done, where he'd failed, where there was minor success. Everything he'd done had been right, but as Kris continued to read, he realized there was a key component missing in every test.

Schooling his features, Kris shrugged. "I don't know.

It's strange. You've done everything, it seems, but I'm not the right person." Except he was. He'd grown up tinkering as much as his father and just because he hadn't studied the same subjects, didn't mean he hadn't a clue.

Blood needed to bind with the chemicals, but the soul needed a will, and the will needed transportation through the bloodstream to keep the soul pumping through the automaton. Magic didn't exist in their world, but religion did, and it didn't take a scholar in religion to garner that information.

It occurred to Kris that he should tell his father this, but the fact that he'd dragged a poor man into the cellar to kill still disgusted him. And the ease with which he'd so carelessly ended the man's life was enough to chase that thought away. His father didn't deserve to know the missing element.

Pressing his lips together, Kris ran his thumb along his brow, smoothing out any suspicious lines that grew. "Do you mind if I take this upstairs to study it a little?" If he could copy the notes and implant his ideas, he could sell it. Damn his parents and their wretched ways. He'd have his own money and he could run with Emilie.

A beat went by, his father's eyes narrowing as he considered it. "Very well. Don't keep them too long. I'm ahead of the game still, no one has cracked this. Automatons with personalities are one thing, but containing a human soul is another entirely."

He was right. Countless individuals were attempting to replicate what someone had done only once. None could find that key, but none thought with more than their mind.

"I'll have the notes back to you, but it'd likely be a good thing for you to take a break away from them. Frustration is the worst block for creativity." He grinned, but it faded quickly as his father didn't show any sign of amusement. With another shrug, he turned on his heel. "I'll see what I can do for you."

In the course of two days, Kris had copied down the notes and implemented his additions. An automaton needed life within it. Nanobots, infused with blood and essence, would carry the soul through the alchemical blood mixture, lending life and soul to the machine. His father would've been proud if he saw the addition, but he never would, because the notes weren't for him.

A crackling on Kris's desk snagged his attention. A small screen glowed gray, then a fuzzy picture grew into focus. Soft blond curls clung to Emilie's skin, and even with the sepia-toned screen, he could tell she was paler than usual.

He knew the doctor would be visiting her today. She hadn't felt right . . . too tired, decreased appetite, and heaviness in her chest.

"Kristoph," Emilie spoke his name softly. "The doctor just left." The words hung in the air for a moment, and she nodded. "It's not looking good. My blood tests are all over the place."

That's not what he wanted to hear, but it was the truth they both had to face. He frowned, dragging a hand through his hair. "I'll find someone to treat you." Desperation clawed at his mind, his heart. He squeezed the pen in his fingers, shaking his head. "I'll do whatever I can for you, Emilie, you know that. If I have to scour the world, I will."

"Kristoph," she murmured, lowering her eyes. "You know what this disease does."

Every muscle in his face tensed. He slammed his fist down on his desk, but his eyes remained soft. He could see them in the reflection on the screen. They were so full of fear, hurt, bitterness, anger. Love. "It won't take you from me. I won't let it, Emilie. We belong together. For always."

Emilie touched her fingers against the screen. "For always." She withdrew her hand, sighing. "I'd like to see you today. Do you think you can?"

Even as Emilie spoke, Kris's mind ran through various scenarios. There was no way that his father would help pay for Emilie's treatments, and even if Kris dipped his fingers into his savings, the moment his father learned of it, he'd surely freeze the accounts.

Uncle Hakon was an option. Unlike Kris's father, Hakon was genuinely kind and possessed a warm heart. Growing up, Kris never had much of a relationship with him, mostly because of his father's prejudices. If he could appeal to him . . .

"How can I deny my lovely rose a visit?" Kris leaned in toward the screen, offering her a smile. "I need to visit someone I haven't seen in a very long time." Tilting his head, he stared through strands of blond. "I'll be over for supper. How is that?"

Emilie's smile grew, adding warmth to her cherubic features. "Lovely. I'll let my parents know an extra plate needs to be set."

"Perfect." He leaned his chin into his palm. "Be sure to save a kiss for me too." Kris could make out the color rushing into her cheeks, which made him grin.

"Kris!" she whisper-yelled at him. "I'll see you soon."

The screen on the device cut out, growing crackly again as the picture faded into grayness. With Emilie not staring at him, his features tightened again. Why, of all people, did his Emilie have to endure Ironbark disease?

Worry weighed him down. He leaned against the back of the chair, stared up at the ceiling, and willed whatever power that lay beyond the heavens to listen. *Help. Help her.*

But if life taught Kris one thing, it was to never wait for someone else to make a move. He shifted, glancing down at the paper that he copied, and scooped up his notebook. It would do no good if his father found it. So he swept it into a drawer on his desk, then locked it.

Hope simmered in his chest. Perhaps his uncle would sympathize with him.

FIVE

Outside of the Sevrein's family home, steam clouded the sky, blocking the sun's midday rays. It was unfortunate, but given the heat the summer sun had been producing, Kris took the reprieve. Amidst the birds twittering in the trees, the low humming of a passing dirigible caught his attention, then the airship came into view, tugging along a banner that read *Thor Industries. Your new employee awaits.* Thor Industries was Agderland's top company as far as automatons—or any steam machine went. Kris's father was hoping to sell them his soul-imbued patent, if that day ever came.

He rounded the corner of the family home and headed toward a detached building set back from the road. It held the family vehicles. Since horses weren't favored transport any longer, most homes had steam-powered cabs. They were cleaner than horses, far easier on expenses, and the upkeep was cheaper, too.

Kris cranked a wheel, which opened the door slowly. When it was finally open, he walked toward his cab. It looked similar to a horse-drawn hackney, except it boasted two wheels in the back and one up front. Where the horse should've stood was a steering wheel, and behind the driver's bench hid the rumbling steam engine.

Moving toward the machine, Kris used the step to haul himself up on the maroon velvet cushion. As he sat, he turned the key, watching as the needle on a gauge flew toward the opposite end, signifying the steam was already bubbling within the water tank. A few more seconds and he turned the engine on. It started with a thunderous rumble, then produced a cloud of steam.

As soon as Kris shifted the vehicle out of park, it took off at a steady puttering on the street. If the streets were clear, he'd be at his uncle's within the hour.

The odds were in his favor. No steam hackneys or trollies cluttered the roadway, but it still took nearly an hour to travel toward the countryside of Skonstad.

The air smelled cleaner, fresher out in the rural part of the city. It had a crisp quality to it that was lacking in the metropolitan area. Kris could nearly taste the icy mountain water on his tongue and it made him yearn for a life out here, rather than the claustrophobic setting of the inner city.

Homes dotted the road, but they didn't overshadow one another. They even possessed more than a note's worth of land to boot. This was what he wanted with Emilie and for their future.

The engine's putting didn't echo off any buildings. It was as if the open air swallowed it up. Kris smiled to himself as he followed the winding road. Fluff from dandelions floated on the breeze in front of him, and he lifted his hand from the wheel to catch some. *Wishes*, he thought. *Emilie always said there were thousands of wishes waiting to be made.*

Opening his hand, he blew as hard as he could, wishing for a lifetime with his beloved rose a thousand times over a thousand.

The machine stuttered as it climbed a hill. Heat from the exhaust wafted over Kris's back, only adding to the sweat that already licked at his brow.

He was nearly there.

Beyond the hill, the Sevrein Estate sat sprawling along its lustrous land. Wildflowers bloomed in various colors, and tall oaks loomed close to the impressive structure.

White-washed stone reflected the sun, temporarily blinding Kris as he looked at it for too long. He had forgotten how unique the mansion was. Spires jutted toward the sky as if they were intent on stabbing it. There were more windows than he could count and on the very top floor, which was the third floor in the house, an expansive balcony stretched across one spire.

Kris steered the steam hackney down the gravel road, which led him into a small courtyard. He cut the engine, then wiped the sweat from his face. Stretching his long legs, he hopped down and walked up to the front door.

Just as he was readying to ring the bell, the door swung open.

No automaton stared at him, but doe-brown eyes set in a middle-aged woman's face did. "Dr. Se—no." She paused, seemingly gathering her wits. Graying blond hair was pulled back into a tight, tidy bun. Recognition dawned on her. "Goodness me, is that you, Lord Kristoph?" Turid, the housekeeper, blinked up at him.

"In the flesh," he said with a grin.

"So I see. Come in." She opened the door wide, allowing him passage. "Your uncle is in his study, if that's who you're here to see."

"It is, actually."

Turid nodded. "Your aunt is in the gardens with the baby."

"Baby?" Kris echoed. Confusion tugged his voice up an octave. *When did Hakon and Saxa have a baby?*

"Yes. Didn't you know? A little girl was born in the spring. Her name is Tindra." Turid waved her hand before placing it on her heart. "The sweetest babe and so good too."

Kris's brows furrowed, but he didn't linger to talk about the newest addition to the family. Unfortunately for Hakon, a little girl wouldn't be inheriting this estate. He frowned, walking through the front hall and toward the breezeway that led to the grand staircase. Upstairs to the right, the study was the first room.

The door was wide open and the first sight he saw was the wall of books. His uncle was at his desk near the massive bay window, head bowed as he read whatever lay in front of him.

Kris rapped his finger on the door frame and waited until his uncle looked up. "Hello, Uncle. I hear congratulations are in order."

Hakon's light-blue eyes lit up. "Kristoph!" He stood from his chair and crossed the room, wasting no time embracing Kris. Unused to such affections, Kris stood awkwardly and patted his uncle on the back. "By the light, I haven't seen you in a while. You look like a man . . . a far more handsome one than your father." He winked.

Kris chuckled. It was odd seeing how light-hearted his uncle could be, while his father was the polar opposite.

"Come, sit." Hakon motioned toward a leather couch against the wall nearest to Kris. The deep red-brown leather complemented the dark-green walls of the study. "Would you care for anything to drink?"

Kris lowered himself, then shook his head. "No, I'm afraid I'm not here for a pleasant reason. I'm here to ask for a favor."

Hakon leaned into the corner of the couch but didn't say a word.

With a frown, Kris continued. "The young woman I wish to marry suffers from Ironbark disease. She's received some troubling news." His hands ran along the top of his knees, then dragged down his thighs. "It's not looking good. There are trial medications out there. If I could tap into my savings then she'd be all set, but I know the moment I do—"

"Your father would freeze the account." Hakon's tone was matter-of-fact, but his familiar eyes held more compassion than Kris expected. "Your father is my brother, but I don't understand him. We were raised the same, and our parents never taught us to be callous or cold." He sighed, scratching between his eyebrows. "I think fear of failure and fear of *life* has warped him. That aside, my boy, I will help you with the treatments, with no strings attached. Sorensen's Pharmaceuticals has created a trial drug. It may be worth considering." He leaned forward, patting Kris's knee. "But tell me something. Are you still into flowers? I need some opinions on the gardens. And while you're out there, you can meet Tindra."

Fatherly pride shone within Hakon's features. He was older than Kris's father and his wife was only a little younger than Kris's mother. Try as they would, it seemed impossible for them to conceive a child—until last year, clearly.

"I did not know you were expecting, but congratulations."

A dark shadow passed over Hakon's eyes, but he said nothing. Kris wondered what it was, if it had to do with Saxa, and what price the child had come at. They were dark musings. But the world wasn't kind to most.

"Thank you." Hakon nodded, then stood from the couch before motioning to Kris. "Let's check out that garden."

For a half hour they milled around the gardens.

Thankfully, Kris hadn't seen his aunt or the baby and thought he was free of that interaction until they rounded the backyard and Kris stopped short before colliding into a body.

A baby with chubby red cheeks blinked up at him from beneath a frilly white bonnet. Kris stared down into the nearly clear blue eyes of the infant, which were so much like his own. Wisps of the lightest shade of blond tickled at her wrinkled forehead.

He'd never proclaimed himself one who enjoyed babies or even knew how to act around them. But she was downright angelic looking.

"You can hold her if you'd like." Saxa shifted Tindra in her arms and offered her to Kris. Before he could refuse, the child had passed from her hands to his.

Awkwardly, Kris held her out, his brows furrowing in discomfort. "Hello, Tindra," he murmured softly, pulling her closer to his chest. She was a robust little thing, able to hold her head up and look around shakily.

It made him wonder, if life were kinder could this ever be a possibility for himself and Emilie? The thought pulled a smile from him and without a word, he returned Tindra to her mother's arms.

"I cannot stay, but I'm sure you'll see me around more often." He bowed his head and continued down the path that led to the courtyard up front. Already, his uncle waited at the machine, tapping on it with his knuckle.

"I don't understand why everything has to be a machine these days." He sighed as he righted himself.

Kris shrugged, propping himself against one of the tall wheels on the rear end of the machine. "It's the way of the world, so it would seem. Humankind complains too much, and they are too self-important to perform various tasks. You rarely hear an automaton complain."

"Spoken like your father." Hakon paused, bowing his head. "I mean no offense, only that he shares a similar view. There is nothing wrong with it."

"I never said I agreed with the view. It's just a fact." Kris's lips thinned as he fought to control a mounting temper. He didn't want to be anything like his father.

Hakon closed the distance between them and planted his hand on Kris's shoulder, squeezing it. "Take care. You have my word that I'll do what I can when you need me. I'll look into Sorensen's trials."

"Thank you again, Uncle." Kris offered a small smile, then climbed into his steam hackney, turned the engine on, and prepared to journey to Emilie's. He had good news at least, and finally someone who would help them.

SIX

On arrival at the Nilssons' home, Kris could already smell the fragrance of almond cake. It was his favorite dessert, and they always made certain he had plenty of it when he stayed for supper.

Halfway to the door, Emilie emerged onto the front porch and held her hand out. "I've been waiting for you." She wore a pale-blue sleeveless dress with ruffles on the shoulders. It clung to her slender frame, which seemed frailer than usual. Kris didn't want to dwell on it, but it was difficult to distract himself from the truth as it glared at him.

He bowed his head as he gently took her hand in his, then placed a tender kiss to her knuckles. "And here I am." Pulling back, he scanned the windows for spying parents, and when he saw nothing, he scooped Emilie into his arms. He squeezed her gently and peppered kisses along her temple. "I'm famished, but after supper we need to talk."

Emilie closed her eyes as Kris continued to kiss every inch of her face, but when his lips connected to hers, she stiffened, then relaxed in his arms. Her soft lips tasted of almond cake and herbal tea.

"Supper is ready," she murmured against his lips and leaned in for another lingering kiss.

Kris shifted his jaw and sighed. "Very well." His broad shoulders slumped as he took one slow step after the other.

Emilie laughed, tugging on his hand. "Come on." She squeezed her fingers against his. "I've saved kisses for after dessert." Glancing up at him through her lashes, she offered a teasing smile.

It was enough to twist his gut with desire. Kris longed to take her into his arms and claim every part of her as his own. To have her take his name, his body, as much as she took his heart.

"Damn good manners to the depths," he proclaimed as he followed her into the house for supper.

By the time they'd finished eating, the sun had dipped below the mountains and the moon ascended to its throne amidst the velvet night sky. Stars twinkled like diamonds in light, mesmerizing Kris. Beside him on a blanket, Emilie leaned against him, staring up at the sky.

He dragged his knuckles down her cheek, then spread his fingers through her pale blond hair. The strands were like threads of moonlight against his skin—like gossamer.

Just as his orchids were delicate, so was Emilie. And yet she was resilient despite what life threw at her.

"I spoke with my uncle." Kris broke the silence. "He agreed to help find treatment. Sorensen Pharmaceuticals has a trial drug . . . "

Emilie withdrew, twisting to face him. Instead of the elation he figured she might display, her brows furrowed in confusion. Almost as if she were displeased. "Kristoph, I don't know."

"Don't know what? It could alleviate all of your symptoms from Ironbark, it could even—" Emilie's fingers against his lips silenced him and a knot of emotion formed in his chest, throbbing. Did she not want to be well? Did she not want to be with him?

"All I've ever wanted is a life with you. But you deserve more, Kristoph. You deserve to not worry if I catch a cold, if it'll be my end. Or if I don't eat a proper meal, if it'll send my body into rebellion. I want that for you because I love you."

He didn't like the tone of her voice, as if she'd all but given up and resigned herself to a shortened lifespan. Frowning, he turned to her and cupped her face. "Emilie, you are my very breath. There will only ever be one you, do you hear me? One you and one love."

She grabbed his wrists, squeezing. "No. There will be more life for you. Understand this: I don't want you to cease living when I draw my last breath. You will continue to live and learn to love again."

Kris didn't understand. Was this her goodbye? "Emilie?"

"I will fight as long as I can, and so I'll try the trial drug, but know this . . . When my time comes . . . let me go." Her voice broke as she spoke the words. Leaning forward, she pressed her forehead against his.

Panic gripped at Kris, and he pulled backward. "Marry me. Not tomorrow, but soon. Marry me."

"Kris, my father . . ." she whispered, withdrawing from him. "You know what he's said, and you know he wants us to wait for my birthday."

He frowned, knowing fully well what her father thought. But maybe with the news he'd be more forgiving. Kris hoped, anyway.

"I'll ask then. I won't know unless I ask . . . again." His lips twisted into a sardonic smile. Could life simply let him have one thing? Just one. He'd give away his wealth and the clothes off his back in trade for Emilie's health.

Emilie sighed, relaxing or simply letting the topic go. She settled into his side once again and before long, she drifted off into a light slumber. Her head rested against his chest as they lay on the blanket. But while she slept, Kris wished on a thousand stars.

A splatter of rain against his cheek disturbed his wishes. There were few clouds in the sky; it was likely a passing cloud. Not wanting to rouse Emilie, he scooped her up into his arms and carried her into the house. She was in a deeper sleep than he thought, for she didn't wake when he ascended the stairwell and brought her into her room.

When Kris came downstairs, Mr. Nilsson nodded. "I think we need to talk." He motioned toward the sitting room, pipe in his other hand.

"Yes, sir, we do." Kris followed him toward the room and sat in a chair. "She was tired."

"And will continue to grow more tired as the days pass." He frowned, opting to stand near the bay window. Rain pelted against it, sending rivulets coursing down the glass. "Her results weren't good today. I know you love her nearly as much as I do, and she feels strongly about you as well—"

"Pardon, Mr. Nilsson, but I'm keen on speaking straightforwardly." Kris ran his hands along his thighs, gripping his knees tightly. Would any of the wishes he made come true? There was one he could test. "I'd like to ask Emilie to be my wife. I know you've said on her eighteenth birthday, but with just under six months to go and with tomorrow not being promised . . ." He clasped his hands together, bowing his head as his throat bobbed with emotion. "With all due respect, I'd like to marry your daughter with or without your blessing."

Mr. Nilsson's lips twitched, his expression unreadable for a moment, and then he laughed. It sounded tired— hollow. "With or without my blessing," he echoed. "Kristoph, you're as much a son to me as Emilie is my daughter. I give you my blessings because I know that every day is a gift."

Kris nodded. "My uncle has agreed to help pay for some treatments. Sorensen has trials for a new drug that allegedly weakens the effects of Ironbark. I told Emilie about it, and she wishes to try it." He omitted the fact that she'd sounded defeated outside, as if the end was already near.

Mr. Nilsson moved away from the window and took a seat in a chair across from Kris. "A trial . . ." His eyes darted toward the ceiling as he sighed. "Thank you." His tone was tight, as if he were trying not to cry. Clearing his throat, he rubbed beneath his eye and tossed his pipe into the dish on the end table near him. "It's raining. Please stay the night in the spare room."

Kris wanted to speak more on it, but Mr. Nilsson's weary expression and the distant look in his eyes told him it was his cue to leave. Even Kris felt exhausted enough to retire to bed early.

Weeks, not days, passed by before Sorensen Pharmaceuticals finally reached out to Emilie about the trials. With only four more months until her birthday, Kris had a lot to think about. He'd nearly paced straight through his bedroom's flooring as he dwelled on what to do. In the end, he commissioned a gold ring with diamonds crafted into a flower.

But with each passing week, it never felt as though it were the right time. Not wanting to waste a minute more, he pocketed the ring box on the day he accompanied Emilie to her appointment.

She stood by his side, wearing a cream-yellow dress with a brown leather belt cinching it. It clung to her frail figure and lent her a ghostly glow. "Do you think this will work?" Emilie's voice came softly. Uncertainty and hopefulness laced her tone.

Kris wanted to say without a doubt it would, but he was ever a pragmatic man. "There is only one way to find out, and if not, think of all the time you get to spend with me." He winked as he slid his hand down her back and to her hip.

She turned to face the building in front of them. It looked more like a church than a pharmaceutical company. Windows lined the first level, spanning from floor to ceiling, and a single spire jutted toward the sky. As long as Kris had been alive, it'd always been Sorensen Pharmaceuticals, but perhaps before then it'd been a place of worship.

"Shall we, my rose?" Kris smiled down at Emilie, and when she nodded, he escorted her into the building.

The inside had vaulted ceilings that didn't argue with the notion that the building was, in fact, a church in a previous life. And the windows that spanned across the walls lent it so much natural lighting, it bleached out the rooms and gave it a sterile feeling. Like a hospital.

"Good afternoon," a woman at the front desk greeted, far too chirpy. Her smile was as white as the uniform dress she wore. "Who is checking in?" She blinked owlishly and glanced between him and Emilie.

"I am." Emilie moved forward and looked down at the sign-in sheet. "Emilie Nilsson," she stated as she wrote her name down.

"Very well. Thank you, Emilie. You may have a seat, and someone will call you." The woman turned her attention to the typewriter in front of her and continued working.

Emilie didn't say a word. She never did when she was nervous. Instead, she picked at her short nails and ran the toe of her boot along the heel of her other foot.

Kris laid his hand on top of hers and squeezed. "I am here. No matter what." He lifted their hands and kissed her fingertips.

She blushed at the show of affection in public, but Kris didn't give one lick about what anyone else thought.

"I just don't want to get my hopes up." She paused, then added, "*Our* hopes."

"Emilie Nilsson," a man's voice called from the hallway. His dark curls were plastered against his head, and it took a moment for Kris to figure out what was so unsettling about him, but then he homed in on it. One eye was a light shade of green, while the other was surrounded with bronze. In the very center, a dark-green iris whirred as it focused on them.

Kris watched in fascination as the mechanical iris expanded then closed of its own accord, adjusting with the lighting of the room. No doubt it was one of Thor Industries' pieces.

Emilie was the first to stand, then Kris followed as she approached the man. "That is me," she offered softly.

The man smiled. "Ah, so good to meet you." He extended his hand in greeting, bowing his head. "I am Dr. Sorensen, the head of the trials, amongst other things."

"Other things, such as running a pharmaceutical company?" Kris's tone was flat. There was something about the man he didn't like and although he couldn't put his finger on it, the gut feeling was there. He lifted a brow and grudgingly shook his hand after Emilie.

"Kristoph Sevrein." Even as he said the name, he could see Sorensen's eyes widen a fraction.

"Magnus's boy," Sorensen stated then turned on his heel, opting not to say any more, which only irritated Kris.

If Sorensen knew his father on a first name basis, it meant they'd shared the same circle at one point. Of course, Kris's father had never spoken about Sorensen outside of whatever was in the paper.

But considering Sorensen was highly successful and Kris's father was still tinkering in their cellar, he could gather why his father never spoke of the doctor.

It was Emilie's turn to squeeze his hand, to calm him.

Dr. Sorensen led them into a room. It didn't look like a typical office room. They had furnished it with an over-sized couch with plush green cushions. A stained glass floor lamp stood next to it. Several rows of ceiling-high bookshelves lined the wall and next to a window sat a leather medical chair.

The doctor motioned toward the couch, and he walked to the desk near the door. "Have a seat." The spot between his brows wrinkled as he glanced down at the file on his desk. "I've had a chance to go over your medical files, Emilie, and . . . your results are alarming."

SEVEN

Kris's heart thundered in his ears. He slid his fingers through Emilie's and squeezed her hand to stop her from picking at her nails. Her rose-colored lips were a sickly pale and the skin beneath her eyes was bruised with shadows.

Had her results differed so greatly from just a few weeks ago?

"I compared yesterday's results to when you first reached out to us, and it's astonishing how rapidly your case is progressing." Dr. Sorensen shook his head and drummed his fingers on his desk. He looked at Emilie like one would a formula or a thesis. She was neither, and Kris wanted to charge him, slam him against the wall, and throttle him.

Was his anger misdirected? Surely, but acting on it might have made him feel better.

Emilie worried at her bottom lip. "What does that mean?"

"It means we need to act quickly. We use the NV1 drug to essentially lull the disease into a deep slumber. Right now, it isn't a fix, just enough to buy us some time to figure out how the drug affects the disease. If we can learn to suppress it . . . we have a hope of creating a new treatment that will effectively put the disease into remission."

Emilie nodded. Although she smiled, Kris could tell it was out of anxiety, not out of politeness or even hope. He couldn't imagine how she felt because he could scarcely grasp the strands of his emotions.

"The first few treatments are administered intravenously, and we would prefer Miss Nilsson stay over for observation."

"I'd like to continue forward," she confirmed, to which Dr. Sorensen replied by offering her a folder of paperwork.

"I'll need you to look over this and sign on the dotted lines."

Emilie glanced over at Kris as if to ask, *Where do we begin?* Kris wished he had the words, but they didn't come. He only hoped that his eyes conveyed, *Here, right here.*

Shakily, she took up a pen, reading along with Kris. Nothing stood out to him as absurd. It was all fairly simple literature stating the company wasn't at fault, this was a trial, and they made no promises as to remission or recovery.

After they read through, Emilie signed the paperwork.

Kris turned his gaze to the doctor. "May we have luncheon before Emilie is admitted?"

"Absolutely. Once you're done, just check in at the desk and we'll be ready for you, Miss Nilsson." Dr.

Sorensen pushed away from his desk and extended his hand to Kris. "We are hopeful that this will work."

Hopeful. Kris gritted his teeth and turned for the door, escorting Emilie out. She cast her eyes downward, remaining far too quiet as they walked down the long hallway.

"What is it?" Kris prompted.

"I'm thankful. It's just . . . what if it's for nothing?" Emilie's voice sounded hollow. "What if . . . I'm taken away from you, anyway?"

To that, Kris had so many words jumbling in his head, but only a few came out. "I'd fight tooth and nail to bring you back."

Emotions swirled within her gaze. Fear, hope, love. But she grew quiet once again and remained so as they walked through the streets of Skonstad.

A dirigible hummed above them, and the faint sound of a loudspeaker from the airship crackled. Another tour for visitors who were passing through or purposely staying in the technological capital of the world.

All of the technology and still no way to stop Ironbark from advancing. Kris's lips tensed into a sneer.

"Oh, look," Emilie began. "They have meatballs at this stand." She tugged him along to the stall, the smell of spices and sauce wafting toward him. The sun beat down on them; it was too hot to eat steaming meatballs, but Emilie wanted them. "Extra lingonberries, please." Her eyes lit up with excitement. The first flash of life he'd seen all day, and it made Kris chuckle that it was for food, of all things.

Across from the food stand, the city park bustled with life. Children flew kites, couples played Kubb on the lawn. Kris picked at his food, not hungry but suddenly anxious. The ring box in his pocket might have been a lead weight for as heavy as it felt.

Leading Emilie to a bench where they could eat, he sat down and set aside his food. For someone usually so composed and unwilling to show his nerves, he was doing a poor job of concealing them. Even Kris knew he was fidgeting.

"Emilie—"

"Kris, are you all right?" She turned to face him, features pinched as suspicion or worry grew.

"I'm all right, I assure you." He slid from the bench, kneeling on the ground. Slowly, he extracted the box from his pocket. "Emilie, I love you no matter what. In sickness, health, better and worse. I will be your champion and fight with and for you." He revealed the ring nestled inside, the diamonds catching the sun's rays enough to make them glitter. "Will you marry me?"

Emilie gasped, clutching her chest. Shock filtered into her gaze, happiness, then she frowned and slid her fingers beneath his chin. "But my father . . . "

Kris's heart roared in his ears at the frown, but his worries faded at her words. "Already handled that. We have his blessing."

Tears shimmered in Emilie's eyes. "Truly?" She dropped her hand, offering it to him instead.

"I have never been so certain of something in my life."

"And I've never been so certain when I say yes." She wiggled her fingers at him, smiling as he slid the ring on. "But promise me this . . . "

"Emilie," he hissed, but her eyes implored him to listen.

"Don't dwell on the bad." Emilie leaned forward and pressed a soft kiss to his lips.

Was that truly what she was going to say? Kris didn't believe it. But he allowed himself to bask in the moment and soak up the goodness that radiated from Emilie.

Every good thing must come to an end, and in Kris's life, goodness never lasted. Emilie's treatments began, and the drug made her ill almost immediately, but her numbers remained steady as far as her lab work went.

The first week, she remained in the Institute. The second week she spent regaining her strength, and the third week she was finally herself again. The color returned to her cheeks, the bruising beneath her eyes lessened, and she longed to use the strength she regained to dance with Kris as she used to.

Kris spent as much time as he possibly could with Emilie, and when he was forced to return home, he did his best to avoid his father.

Unfortunately, he couldn't avoid his father on a particularly wretched afternoon. A gnawing anxiousness had hatched within Kris, growing with each passing day. His father always seemed to amplify this, so when he sat at the breakfast table with a smug look on his face, Kris knew a storm brewed.

"You're wasting your time and efforts with that girl." It was the same tiresome insult repeatedly. When Kris said nothing and only crammed a piece of bacon in his mouth, his father continued, "She'll be dead next month."

That was it. Kris slammed his fists on the table, bolting from his seat to loom over his plate. "Shut your mouth, you old coot. You know nothing of Emilie's health."

Magnus scooped his spoon up nonchalantly and dug into his fruit bowl. "On the contrary, I know everything about her health." His eyes narrowed as he looked at his son. "Did you know that before I married your mother, Vidar Sorensen had been vying for her hand?" He shook his head, sighing. "He was the top of the class in our university days, and I was second to him, but I won your mother in the end."

What relevance did this have? Kris rolled his eyes as his father took a stroll down memory lane, which only served to frustrate him further. "I don't care about your glory days."

"You should because, you see, Vidar told me that you're paying for Emilie's treatments, which isn't true because you haven't touched your accounts. So that means you're getting money from somewhere else, and a little birdy told me that my traitorous brother is doing that. How clever of you, Kristoph."

Kris shoved the chair out of his way, readying to leave the room and not play his father's sordid game, but then his father spoke again.

"Emilie will be dead by the end of summer. I don't know what lies Vidar is feeding you, but her numbers are plummeting rapidly. He needs the funds to continue the trials, but her chemistry has rejected the drug." The smug look remained on his face, his unrepentant words like a dagger to the heart.

"You lie." Kris's voice came in a harsh whisper.

His father sat there, so composed, so calm . . .

"No. I spoke to him yesterday about treatment for your mother, and imagine my surprise when he mentioned seeing my son." He waved his hand toward Kris.

Rage boiled over and before Kris knew it, he stood in front of his father, fists clenching the front of his shirt. "Then why didn't he tell us? You're lying!"

His father's brows dipped downward, and his face turned a deep crimson. "I am not! Her kidneys are shutting down—already, her heart is weakening."

A low keening emitted from Kris as he slammed his father back against the chair. He didn't want to believe him. He wanted it to be a wicked lie, but there was no tell showing at his father's jaw or eye.

Relinquishing his hold on him, Kris withdrew and turned his back to his father. "If what you say is true,

Sorensen will never forget my name." He quickly exited the dining room, rubbing at his eyes as tears burned them.

Kris moved his hand to his chest. It ached as if someone were twisting his heart. He realized he was sucking in breath rapidly, and he sank to his knees. He splayed his hands on the black-and-white tile, gasping for breath that wouldn't come.

Emilie couldn't die. She was his love, his light. Everything that was good in him.

He lifted a hand to swipe at a trail of tears, then swallowed them back and stood to his feet. There would be time for tears, but for now . . . Sorensen needed to be dealt with.

EIGHT

Upon arrival at the pharmaceutical company, Kris stormed inside, ignoring the woman at the desk, and charged straight for Sorensen's office. He was nearly there when Mr. Nilsson approached him, his eyes bloodshot, as if he'd been crying.

"Kristoph?" he asked softly. "We tried reaching you. It's Emilie . . . she collapsed at home and we rushed her here."

"Emilie," Kris rasped. "Where?" He followed him down the hall and rushed into the room. Emilie was already hooked up to several lines, one of which pumped fluids into her. She was awake, looking out the window, but her cheeks were hollow and the light in her gaze seemed clouded. He eased toward the bed and grasped her hand. "My rose . . ."

Kris had been so focused on hope that he hadn't noticed how her skin had returned to its gray pallor, or that the bruising beneath her eyes had returned. She was declining and if he hadn't been so foolish or ignorant, perhaps another course could've been taken.

Emilie lifted her other hand, placing it on his. The ring on her finger gleamed in the bright light of the room, seemingly mocking Kris. "You came."

"Of course I did. I'll always come for you." He leaned down, pressing a kiss to her brow. It was cool to the touch. Frowning, Kris peered over his shoulder as metal met the tile flooring.

A whir, then a click as a nurse automaton entered the room. "It is time for your vital check," came the tinny voice. With another series of clicks and whirring, the androgynous figure rounded the hospital bed.

"Isn't the doctor coming in?" Kris asked tightly.

"No." The nurse didn't look at him and its cool tone raked along his nerves, only adding fuel to the fire burning below the surface.

"No?" he asked incredulously and stiffened. "I'll be back, Emilie, get some rest." He bent to kiss her again, glaring at the automaton, then bolted out of the room, not bothering to look at the weeping Mrs. Nilsson.

No doubt they knew the truth or something close to it. The one time Kris wished his father spouted lies was now.

Charging down the hallway, he swung Sorensen's office door open with such force it slammed into the wall, puncturing it with the doorknob. He was ready and caught it as it kicked back toward him. Sorensen leaped up from his seat, recognition dawning on his face. He was tense, his fingers curling toward his palms as he stood, much like a caged animal.

Kris's tall and lean figure dwarfed Sorensen. There was nowhere for him to go, except for calling for security, but as Kris launched over the desk, he curled his fingers around the doctor's white coat and slammed him against the wooden surface.

"You insolent fool," Kris snarled as he yanked the man up, only to smash him down against the desk again. "You knew . . . you knew all along." He could scarcely hear the bellowing coming from Sorensen as he continued to smash him against the desk. Finally, Kris shoved him with enough force that he fell against the wall.

Blood streamed down Sorensen's face and into his mouth. "I did, but it's for the greater good."

"The greater good," Kris echoed, curling his fingers into his palm. He shook with all the rage that had built within him. "I'm tired of hearing what is or isn't for the greater good. You've filled my head with lies and given not only me but Emilie false hope as well. All for what . . . money?"

Sorensen held a hand out. "Stop. It isn't just for money. That money is fueling research for NV1 to improve the success rate."

"No more lies, Sorensen. My father told me you're taking more than just our money. Selling lies and hope to anyone desperate enough to believe it." Kris paced back and forth, jamming his fingers into his hair. "I will ruin you. I will bring your company down . . . " His eyes dropped to the floor, where a cracked picture frame looked up at him. Kris bent over and picked it up. In the sepia-toned picture, he saw Sorensen and a curly-headed boy around the age of seven. "You will be a curse to your son. Shame will follow him and you like a shadow."

He threw the picture frame against the wall then turned his back to the doctor. "Is it true she won't last through the summer?" Kris didn't hear any shuffling, but he cursed as something smashed against the side of his head.

A hot stream flowed over his eyes and when he touched it, blood came away on his fingers. He pivoted on his heel and grabbed Sorensen by the throat, squeezing hard. It would have been so easy to snuff the life out of him.

Sorensen squeaked, gagged, and attempted to claw at Kris's face.

"I didn't hear you, Sorensen. Is it true?" Kris squeezed harder, then tossed him to the floor. Now that his vocal cords were inflamed, he wouldn't be able to talk. *Damn it all.* He glanced down at Sorensen and caught him nodding quickly.

"Dr. Sorensen," a robotic voice called. "Patient Nilsson —" The automaton glanced around the room, assessing the situation before zeroing in on Kris. "I'll page security."

"Don't." Kris took a threatening step forward. "What about Nilsson?"

"She is in heart failure. Kidney function is critically low and her heart—" The automaton couldn't finish because Kris shoved it out of the room and into the hallway wall.

He ran back to Emilie's room and rushed to her bedside. Although his anger didn't subside, it moved out of the way as grief blossomed and lodged a sob in his throat. "Why you?" Kris sat on the bed next to her, lowering his head against her shoulder. "Why not me? I cannot live without you."

Emilie's arm wrapped around his back, and she lifted a hand to cup his cheek. "Yes you can, and you will. You've been the best part of my life for as long as I've known you." She touched the blood on his face, frowning. "I need you to live for me, for the both of us. Do you understand?" She used the sleeve of her gown to wipe away the droplets of blood. "Don't fall back on anger. You're better than that. I love you."

But he wasn't. Kris knew that. Anger gnawed at him like a beast trying to escape its cage.

"It isn't fair." He cupped her hand in both of his and kissed her knuckles. "We belong together." Her eyes fluttered shut and her body relaxed into the mound of pillows behind her as she dozed.

A thought scraped at Kris's mind. If the life he had mapped out with Emilie didn't come to pass, then he would craft a semblance of one himself.

In a matter of days, Emilie's health declined so steadily that he was certain this was the end. However, as evenly tempered as Emilie was, she was stubborn through and through and the way her body clung to life was a sign of that. She wanted to live—she had the will to live.

As the nurse automaton clanked into the room, it assessed Emilie's vitals. "Patient Nilsson won't be waking. We offer our condolences." It paused for a moment, its amber eyes blinking rapidly. "I've contacted her parents." With that, the cool creature left the room.

This was it . . . Kris crawled into the bed next to Emilie, his arms embracing her tightly as he buried his face in her neck. "Please don't leave me. I cannot bear it. I love you . . . " His voice cracked as he dissolved into a fit of sobs.

How long he laid there with his arms around Emilie, he didn't know. He'd been able to say goodbye, but as her fighting body still lay there, unwilling to pass, a thought niggled at him again.

Kris glanced around the room. The Nilssons would return soon, but for now the room was empty, leaving him alone. In the corner of the room sat a phlebotomist's cart. Small vacuum-sealed containers lined the top of the tray, and sterile needles were wrapped in cloth.

"I will have you, one way or another, my rose. Perhaps not as I intended . . . " Rigidly, Kris scooped up a tube, a needle, and a strap. With one more glance to the door, he turned to Emilie. "We will be together again." He set the vacuum container in place, adjusting the needle before he drew Emilie's blood. Once he was through, he pressed a soft kiss to her cool lips and tasted her for the last time.

Kris pocketed the container and left the room.

He hadn't been home in days. Listening to his father laugh or proclaim that he was right hadn't been on the top of Kris's list. There was no part of him that wanted to deal with his father's callous behavior or his mother's moods if she was awake long enough.

But now he needed his father's cellar and the tools within.

Charging into his room, he pulled out the hidden notebook. Immediately, a shadow formed on his bedroom floor, and a knot grew in his stomach.

"The prodigal son returns." His father scoffed. "What did you do to Sorensen? He canceled your mother's treatment." It sounded more like an inconvenience to him than anything. Not that Magnus actually worried for his wife, or about what would happen if she continued to abuse her medication.

"What he had coming to him." Kris shoved past his father but growled as he was yanked back. They stood eye to eye, glowering at one another. "I don't care what happens to that woman. She has never once been a mother to me. You're barely a father to me, so let's hope what I'm about to do works, and then for once in your life, you'd have done something for me."

Magnus's eyes widened. "What?" Glancing down at the notebook in Kris's grasp, he sneered. "Did you steal my notebook?"

"No, I made notes of my own." Kris stripped his sports

jacket off and tossed it across his bedroom, then stormed out into the hall. He gripped the notebook under his armpit and rolled up the sleeves to his shirt. The sound of his shoes slapping against the tile resonated in the quiet house.

"You did what?"

"You wanted me to glance over your notes, so I did. And I found some inconsistencies and had theories of my own. I suppose we'll see if it works." Kris ignored his father the rest of the way into the cellar. Of course the lamps were lit; he'd likely been in his hole when Kris had arrived.

But Kris wasn't here to set his father in his pram and entertain him. He set to searching for the nanobots his father stored away. The ones he found resembled pollywogs. Tails stuck out from behind the rounded bodies, which would propel them through the fluid running through the automaton. But the tiny bots needed a life force infused with them, too.

Pulling out the cylinder of blood, Kris carefully injected the entire container of bots with the fluid. Once completed, he turned to the automaton, which hung limply from the ceiling. His father had repaired it over the weeks.

"If this works, it belongs to me." Kris narrowed his eyes on his father, who nodded emphatically. "Where is the alchemical fluid?"

His father grabbed the oversized beaker of fluid and dropped it in front of Kris, who scooped up the nanobots then plunged them into the liquid.

Kris waited a moment then retrieved the remote that controlled the bots. His heart thundered wildly. Every nerve was on end, because if this worked . . .

He carried the beaker toward the automaton and poured the contents into the tube connected to it. The muddy liquid zig-zagged through the line until it collected inside the automaton's belly.

"Breathe," he said to himself, then pushed the button on the remote. Perhaps the universe smiled at him that day, or maybe it was the thousands of wishes made on dandelions and stars. Kris would say it was fate rewarding him.

As he pressed the button, the automaton whirred to life. Not with jerky movements, but with as much grace as the model could muster. Its eyes, unlike the amber glow they had been before, were a soft blue. Kris hadn't replaced the bulbs and surely his father hadn't either.

A string of curses emitted from his father. "You did it!"

"Wh-what is my name?" the automaton craned its head to look at Kris then at his father, its metallic mouth slanting into a smile. Its voice was female, but it didn't sound like the one he yearned to hear, which was likely for the best.

"Your name . . . " Kris choked out, "is Rose." *His sweet rose.* And yet not. This machine wasn't Emilie, and he knew that, but he'd successfully fused the automaton with a human. What that meant, he didn't know.

"Rose. I like that. But am I prickly?" it asked, so curious, so sweet. So like Emilie.

Kris couldn't help himself. He reached out to touch the automaton's cheek. It looked him in the eyes as if some part of it—her—recognized him. "No. I am the prickly one, thorns and all."

After the exchange, he unplugged Rose from the wires, allowing her body to clunk to the floor. She landed on her feet, unsteady at first, then she found her center.

This was different from the horror Kris had witnessed with the automaton before. This one had been imbued with a part of Emilie.

"I cannot believe you did that," his father said from behind him. "How?"

Kris shifted his jaw. He leveled a glare at his father. "You'll never know, because you will not be the one claiming my work." As soon as the crisp words left his lips, his father's face grew red once more. Perhaps his father longed to shake him senseless, but even he knew better than to push Kris right now.

"Don't be so cross with me, boy. It was your uncle who referred you to Sorensen, after all. He isn't as pristine as you think."

Some people were born skilled weavers, others poets, but Kris's father was born with a barbed tongue that he knew how to wield. He used it to plant noxious seeds within a person. Even if Kris thought nothing of his desperate attempt to rile him and turn him against another in that moment, it would later prove successful on Magnus's part.

"Rose," Kris called softly. "Come with me." He collected the cylinder, notebook, and anything his father may want to peer into, then left the cellar. Behind him, the soft clicking whirrs of the automaton moving followed him.

At the top of the stairs, the head housekeeper frowned at him. "You had a phone call a moment ago . . . It's Emilie, she . . . Oh, I'm so sorry, Master Kristoph . . . She's gone." Ebba dabbed her eyes with a tissue. "Such a beautiful soul she was."

If Kris had known she'd pass so soon, he'd never have left her. A knot lodged itself in his throat, and he closed his eyes. A hand lighted on his shoulder, but it held no warmth. Instead, it was cool.

"Prickly one, are you all right? I sense . . . a sizable amount of sadness in you." Rose shifted, tilting her head to better look at Kris's profile.

Perhaps it was his imagination, but he almost heard an inflection of emotion within her voice. "No. I'm not." Kris waited to see if Rose would act, but silence stretched between them. "I've lost someone very special."

"Do you require assistance finding them?" It was an innocent question, and it held so much damnable hope. As if Rose could bring back Emilie as simple as that. Tears burned his eyes at the thought.

Turning to face Rose, he gazed into the illuminated blue eyes. They weren't Emilie's for they weren't mismatched, or even human-like, but they shone with more concern than his father had ever shown him.

"You won't be able to find her, Rose. Not where she went." Kris pinched the bridge of his nose, squeezing his eyes shut as fresh tears streamed down his cheeks.

"Oh. I am here if you need my help." She stepped beside him, her metal frame still shorter than him.

What came next was something Kris wished he didn't have to do: he needed to see Emilie and the Nilssons. With a funeral now on the horizon, there was much to be planned, and Kris wanted none of it.

But he was there for the Nilssons, who had shown him far more love than his parents ever had, and he was there for Emilie's funeral. Where they played her favorite high-spirited song on a harpsichord and threw rose petals onto her coffin.

Kris had been present for it all, and the one moment he wished he wasn't was when Mr. Nilsson placed the rose diamond ring in his palm.

"She loved you so," was all he said.

And what more could Kris say to that? Because he knew with all his heart how much she loved him, how much he loved her.

Still, it wasn't enough.

EPILOGUE

In the weeks after Emilie's passing, Kris turned his attention away from the solarium, proclaiming to Rose it was a bitter reminder of what no longer was. She didn't understand, but when he'd explained it, she yearned to know more of a human's complex emotions.

It hadn't been exactly what he wanted to hear, but he indulged the curious automaton and divulged as much as he could, answering questions as she spat them out.

Despite how much Kris detested his father's obsession with mechanical things, it was what occupied most of his days. He'd gone out and purchased the latest artificial flesh for Rose, opting to use a sun-kissed complexion. Then came the dark-blond wig that he strategically glued onto her scalp. By the time Kris was finished, Rose looked as human as possible. But her eyes still weren't quite right.

For a week straight, he tinkered in his room until he fashioned the robotic eyes to perfection. When he placed them into her sockets, she blinked slowly, lowering the lashes he'd attached.

"Do I look pretty?" Rose asked, using her smooth voice that Kris had worked on too.

For the first time in weeks, he smiled. She was beautiful. "Very much so." She smiled at him, which twisted his heart. Rose looked so much like Emilie, and yet not. Emilie without the weight of Ironbark, without the exhaustion and not knowing if she'd live to see another day.

"Now what?" Rose ran one of her fingers along the frill of her dress's sleeve.

The smile Kris wore vanished. "Now, we uphold my promise and ensure Sorensen falls. And we'll pay a brief visit to my uncle too."

Elle Beaumont loves creating vivid fantasy and science fiction worlds. She lives in southeastern Massachusetts with her husband and two children. When not writing or chasing around her children she can enjoys making candles. More than once she has proclaimed that coffee is life blood and it is how she refrains from becoming a zombie.

CONNECT WITH ELLE

www.ellebeaumontbooks.com

facebook.com/ellebeaumontbooks

instagram.com/ellebeaumontbooks

bookbub.com/authors/elle-beaumont

Stay up to date and receive some free books by signing up for her newsletter! ellebeaumontbooks.com/newsletter

Join Elle's Facebook group and hang out with her facebook.com/groups/ElleBeaumontStreetTeam

MORE FROM ELLE BEAUMONT

Standalones

Die From A Broken Heart

The Dragon's Bride

The Castle of Thorns (Nov '21)

Gods Among Us

Apple of Fate

Demons of Frosteria

Frost Mate (Dec '21)

Immortal Realms Trilogy

Seeds of Sorrow (coming 2022)

Tides of Torment (coming 2022)

Wages of War (coming 2022)

Music & Wraiths

The Spirit of You

The Hunter Series

Hunter's Truce

Royal's Vow

Assassin's Gambit

Queen's Edge

Baron Weaver Series

Game of Bezique

Secrets of Galathea

Brotherhood of the Sea

Bindings of the Sea

Voice of the Sea

King of the Sea

Anthologies

Of The Deep

Blood From A Stone

Cirque de vol Mystique

Link by Link

Something in the Shadows

Stories For Nerds (Oct '21)

MORE BOOKS YOU'LL LOVE

If you enjoyed this anthology, please consider leaving a review!

Then check out more anthologies from Midnight Tide Publishing!

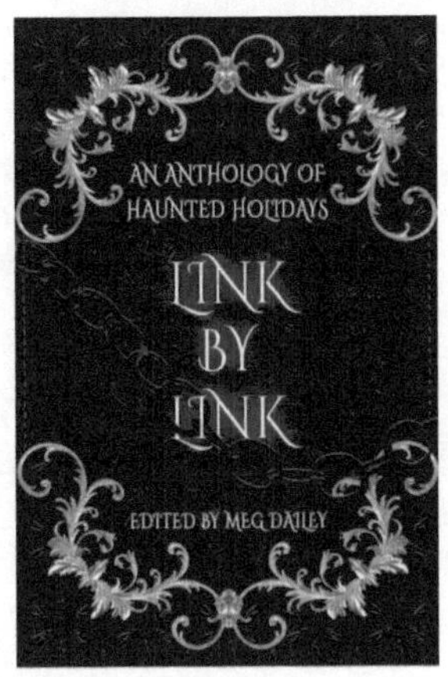

"'I wear the chain I forged in life,' replied the Ghost. 'I made it link by link . . . '"-Charles Dickens, A Christmas Carol.

Link by Link is a collection of 9 stories of ghosts, spirits, and creatures unnamed, all come to teach lessons we won't soon forget. From sweet Christmas tales to terrifying holiday hauntings, these stories take a dive into the past in the hopes of creating a better-or at least different-future.

Available Now

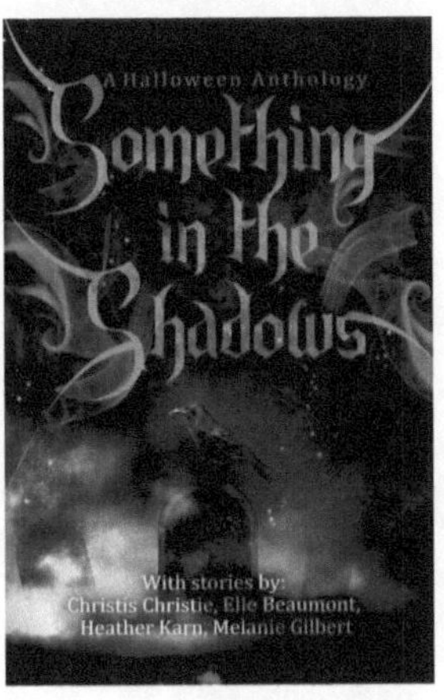

For fans of Moon Called, True Blood, and Vampire Diaries. You've heard their folktales–saw the carnage they left behind–those creatures, the things lurking deep in the shadows, watching and waiting until the right moment to ensnare its prey. Four authors dared to tell their stories in this unique collection of wonderfully haunting and frightful thrillers, and even dark romance. Inside, you'll discover tales of vampires, demons, and humans encountering spirits in these short stories that are sure to keep you up at night!

Available Now

www.ingramcontent.com/pod-product-compliance
Lightning Source LLC
Chambersburg PA
CBHW060928190726
48286CB00002B/677